PERPETUA. A TALE OF NIMES IN A.D. 213

Published @ 2017 Trieste Publishing Pty Ltd

ISBN 9780649669318

Perpetua. A Tale of Nimes in A.D. 213 by S. Baring-Gould

Except for use in any review, the reproduction or utilisation of this work in whole or in part in any form by any electronic, mechanical or other means, now known or hereafter invented, including xerography, photocopying and recording, or in any information storage or retrieval system, is forbidden without the permission of the publisher, Trieste Publishing Pty Ltd, PO Box 1576 Collingwood, Victoria 3066 Australia.

All rights reserved.

Edited by Trieste Publishing Pty Ltd.
Cover @ 2017

This book is sold subject to the condition that it shall not, by way of trade or otherwise, be lent, re-sold, hired out, or otherwise circulated without the publisher's prior consent in any form or binding or cover other than that in which it is published and without a similar condition including this condition being imposed on the subsequent purchaser.

www.triestepublishing.com

S. BARING-GOULD

PERPETUA. A TALE OF NIMES IN A.D. 213

Trieste

PERPETUA

A TALE OF NIMES IN A.D. 213

BY THE
REV. S. BARING-GOULD, M.A.

NEW YORK
E. P. DUTTON & COMPANY
31 WEST TWENTY-THIRD STREET
1897

CONTENTS

CHAPTER	PAGE
I. Est	1
II. Æmilius	14
III. Baudillas, the Deacon	22
IV. The Utriculares	33
V. The Lagoons	45
VI. The Passage into Life	57
VII. Oblations	68
VIII. The Voice at Midnight	81
IX. Stars in Water	93
X. Locutus Est!	105
XI. Palanquins	117
XII. Reus	128
XIII. Ad Fines	140
XIV. To the Lowest Depth	152
XV. "Revealed Unto Babes"	165

CONTENTS

CHAPTER	PAGE
XVI. DOUBTS AND DIFFICULTIES	177
XVII. PEDO	189
XVIII. IN THE CITRON-HOUSE	204
XIX. MARCIANUS	218
XX. IN THE BASILICA	230
XXI. A MANUMISSION	242
XXII. THE ARENA	256
XXIII. THE CLOUD-BREAK	270
XXIV. CREDO	287

PERPETUA

A TALE OF NÎMES IN A.D. 213

CHAPTER I

EST

The Kalends (first) of March.

A brilliant day in the town of Nemausus—the modern Nîmes—in the Province of Gallia Narbonensis, that arrogated to itself the title of being *the* province, a title that has continued in use to the present day, as distinguishing the olive-growing, rose-producing, ruin-strewn portion of Southern France, whose fringe is kissed by the blue Mediterranean.

Not a cloud in the nemophyla-blue sky. The sun streamed down, with a heat that was unabsorbed, and with rays unshorn by any intervenient vapor, as in our northern clime. Yet a cool air from the distant snowy Alps touched, as with the kiss of a vestal, every heated brow, and refreshed it.

The Alps, though invisible from Nemausus, make

themselves felt, now in refreshing breezes, then as raging icy blasts.

The anemones were in bloom, and the roses were budding. Tulips spangled the vineyards, and under the olives and in the most arid soil, there appeared the grape hyacinth and the star of Bethlehem.

At the back of the white city stands a rock, the extreme limit of a spur of the Cebennæ, forming an amphitheatre, the stones scrambled over by blue and white periwinkle, and the crags heavy with syringa and flowering thorns.

In the midst of this circus of rock welled up a river of transparent bottle-green water, that filled a reservoir, in which circled white swans.

On account of the incessant agitation of the water, that rose in bells, and broke in rhythmic waves against the containing breastwork, neither were the swans mirrored in the surface, nor did the white temple of Nemausus reflect its peristyle of channeled pillars in the green flood.

This temple occupied one side of the basin; on the other, a little removed, were the baths, named after Augustus, to which some of the water was conducted, after it had passed beyond the precinct within which it was regarded as sacred.

It would be hard to find a more beautiful scene, or see such a gay gathering as that assembled near the Holy Fountain on this first day of March.

Hardly less white than the swans that dreamily swam in spirals, was the balustrade of limestone that surrounded the sheet of heaving water. At intervals on this breasting stood pedestals, each supporting a statue in Carrara marble. Here was Diana in buskins, holding a bow in her hand, in the attitude of running, her right hand turned to draw an arrow from the quiver at her back. There was the Gallic god Camulus, in harness, holding up a six-rayed wheel, all gilt, to signify the sun. There was a nymph pouring water from her urn; again appeared Diana contemplating her favorite flower, the white poppy.

But in the place of honor, in the midst of the public walk before the fountain, surrounded by acacias and pink-blossomed Judas trees, stood the god Nemausus, who was at once the presiding deity over the fountain, and the reputed founder of the city. He was represented as a youth, of graceful form, almost feminine, and though he bore some military insignia, yet seemed too girl-like and timid to appear in war.

The fountain had, in very truth, created the city. This marvelous upheaval of a limpid river out of the heart of the earth had early attracted settlers to it, who had built their rude cabins beside the stream and who paid to the fountain divine honors. Around it they set up a circle of rude stones, and called the place *Nemet*—that is to say, the Sacred Place. After a while came Greek settlers, and they introduced a new civilization and new ideas. They at once erected an image of the deity of the fountain, and called this deity Nemausios. The spring had been female to the Gaulish occupants of the settlement; it now became male, but in its aspect the deity still bore indications of feminine origin. Lastly the place became a Roman town. Now beautiful statuary had taken the place of the monoliths of unhewn stone that had at one time bounded the sacred spring.

On this first day of March the inhabitants of Nemausus were congregated near the fountain, all in holiday costume.

Among them ran and laughed numerous young girls, all with wreaths of white hyacinths or of narcissus on their heads, and their clear musical voices rang as bells in the fresh air.

Yet, jocund as the scene was, to such as looked

closer there was observable an under-current of alarm that found expression in the faces of the elder men and women of the throng, at least in those of such persons as had their daughters flower-crowned.

Many a parent held the child with convulsive clasp, and the eyes of fathers and mothers alike followed their darlings with a greed, as though desirous of not losing one glimpse, not missing one word, of the little creature on whom so many kisses were bestowed, and in whom so much love was centered.

For this day was specially dedicated to the founder and patron of the town, who supplied it with water from his unfailing urn, and once in every seven years on this day a human victim was offered in sacrifice to the god Nemausus, to ensure the continuance of his favor, by a constant efflux of water, pure, cool and salubrious.

The victim was chosen from among the daughters of the old Gaulish families of the town, and the victim was selected from among girls between the ages of seven and seventeen. Seven times seven were bound to appear on this day before the sacred spring, clothed in white and crowned with spring flowers. None knew which would be chosen and which rejected. The selection was not made by either the priests or the priestesses attached to the temple. Nor was it made by the magistrates of Nemausus. No parent might redeem his child. Chance or destiny alone determined who was to be chosen out of the forty-nine who appeared before the god.

Suddenly from the temple sounded a blast of horns, and immediately the peristyle (colonnade) filled with priests and priestesses in white, the former with wreaths of silvered olive leaves around their heads, the latter crowned with oak leaves of gold foil.

The trumpeters descended the steps. The crowd fell back, and a procession advanced. First came players on the double flute, or syrinx, with red bands round their hair. Then followed dancing girls performing graceful movements about the silver image of the god that was borne on the shoulders of four maidens covered with spangled veils of the finest oriental texture. On both sides paced priests with brazen trumpets.

Before and behind the image were boys bearing censers that diffused aromatic smoke, which rose and spread in all directions, wafted by the soft air that spun above the cold waters of the fountain.

Behind the image and the dancing girls marched

the priests and priestesses, singing alternately a hymn to the god.

"Hail, holy fountain, limpid and eternal,
Green as the sapphire, infinite, abundant,
Sweet, unpolluted, cold and clear as crystal,
   Father Nemausus.

Hail, thou Archegos, founder of the city,
Crowned with oak leaves, cherishing the olive,
Grapes with thy water annually flushing,
   Father Nemausus.

Thou to the thirsty givest cool refreshment,
Thou to the herdsman yieldeth yearly increase,
Thou from the harvest wardest off diseases,
   Father Nemausus.

Seven are the hills on which old Rome is founded,
Seven are the hills engirdling thy fountain,
Seven are the planets set in heaven ruling,
   Father Nemausus.

Thou, the perennial, lovest tender virgins,
Do thou accept the sacrifice we offer;
May thy selection be the best and fittest,
   Father Nemausus."

Then the priests and priestesses drew up in lines between the people and the fountain, and the ædile of the city, standing forth, read out from a roll the names of seven times seven maidens; and as each name was called, a white-robed, flower-crowned child fluttered from among the crowd and was received by the priestly band.

When all forty-nine were gathered together, then they were formed into a ring, holding hands, and round this ring passed the bearers of the silver image.

Now again rose the hymn:

> "Hail, holy fountain, limpid and eternal,
> Green as the sapphire, infinite, abundant,
> Sweet, unpolluted, cold and clear as crystal,
> Father Nemausus."

And as the bearers carried the image round the circle, suddenly a golden apple held by the god, fell and touched a graceful girl who stood in the ring.

"Come forth, Lucilla," said the chief priestess. "It is the will of the god that thou speak the words. Begin."

Then the damsel loosed her hands from those she held, stepped into the midst of the circle and raised the golden pippin. At once the entire ring of children began to revolve, like a dance of white butterflies in early spring; and as they swung from right to left, the girl began to recite at a rapid pace a jingle of words in a Gallic dialect, that ran thus:

"One and two
Drops of dew,
Three and four
Shut the door."

As she spoke she indicated a child at each numeral.

"Five and six
Pick up sticks,
Seven and eight
Thou must wait."

Now there passed a thrill through the crowd, and the children whirled quicker.

"Nine and ten
Pass again.
Golden pippin, lo! I cast,
Thou, Alcmene, touched at last."

At the word "last" she threw the apple and struck a girl, and at once left the ring, cast her coronet of narcissus into the fountain and ran into the crowd. With a gasp of relief she was caught in the arms of her mother, who held her to her heart, and sobbed with joy that her child was spared. For her, the risk was past, as she would be over age when the next septennial sacrifice came round.

Now it was the turn of Alcmene.

She held the ball, paused a moment, looking about her, and then, as the troop of children revolved, she rattled the rhyme, and threw the pippin at a damsel named Tertiola. Whereupon she in turn cast her garland, that was of white violets, into the fountain, and withdrew.

Again the wreath of children circled and Tertiola repeated the jingle till she came to "Touched at last," when a girl named Ælia was selected, and came into the middle. This was a child of seven, who was shy and clung to her mother. The mother fondled her, and said, " My Ælia! Rejoice that thou art not the fated victim. The god has surrendered thee to me. Be speedy with the verse, and I will give thee *crustulæ* that are in my basket."

So encouraged, the frightened child rattled out some lines, then halted; her memory had failed, and she had to be reminded of the rest. At last she also was free, ran to her mother's bosom and was comforted with cakes.

A young man with folded arms stood lounging

near the great basin. He occasionally addressed a shorter man, a client apparently, from his cringing manner and the set smile he wore when addressing or addressed by the other.

"By Hercules!" said the first. "Or let me rather swear by Venus and her wayward son, the Bow-bearer, that is a handsome girl yonder, she who is the tallest, and methinks the eldest of all. What is her name, my Callipodius?"

"She that looks so scared, O supremity of excellent youths, Æmilius Lentulus Varo! I believe that she is the daughter and only child of the widow Quincta, who lost her husband two years ago, and has refused marriage since. They whisper strange things concerning her."

"What things, thou tittle-tattle bearer?"

"Nay, I bear but what is desired of me. Didst thou not inquire of me who the maiden was? I have a mind to make no answer. But who can deny anything to thee?"

"By the genius of Augustus," exclaimed the patron, "thou makest me turn away my head at thy unctuous flattery. The peasants do all their cooking in oil, and when their meals be set on the table the appetite is taken away, there is too much oil. It is so with thy conversation. Come, thy news."

"I speak but what I feel. But see how the circle is shrunk. As to the scandal thou wouldst hear, it is this. The report goes that the widow and her daughter are infected with a foreign superstition, and worship an ass's head."

"An ass's head hast thou to hold and repeat such lies. Look at the virgin. Didst ever see one more modest, one who more bears the stamp of sound reason and of virtue on her brow. The next thou wilt say is——"

"That these Christians devour young children."

"This is slander, not scandal. By Jupiter Camulus! the circle is reduced to four, and she, that fair maid, is still in it. There is Quinctilla, the daughter of Largus; look at him, how he eyes her with agony in his face! There is Vestilia Patercola. I would to the gods that the fair—what is her name?"

"Perpetua, daughter of Aulus Har——"

"Ah!" interrupted the patron, uneasily. "Quinctilla is out."

"Her father, Aulus Harpinius——"

"See, see!" again burst in the youth Æmilius,

"there are but two left; that little brown girl, and she whom thou namest———"

"Perpetua."

Now arrived the supreme moment—that of the final selection. The choosing girl, in whose hand was the apple, stood before those who alone remained. She began:

> "One, two
> Drops of dew."

Although there was so vast a concourse present, not a sound could be heard, save the voice of the girl repeating the jingle, and the rush of the holy water over the weir. Every breath was held.

> "Nine and ten,
> Pass again.
> Golden pippin, now I cast,
> Thou, Portumna, touched at last."

At once the brown girl skipped to the basin, cast in her garland, and the high priestess, raising her hand, stepped forward, pointed to Perpetua, and cried, "Est."

CHAPTER II

ÆMILIUS

When the lot had fallen, then a cry rang from among the spectators, and a woman, wearing the white cloak of widowhood, would have fallen, had she not been caught and sustained by a man in a brown tunic and *lacerna* (short cloak).

"Be not overcome, lady," said this man in a low tone. "What thou losest is lent to the Lord."

"Baudillas," sobbed the woman, "she is my only child, and is to be sacrificed to devils."

"The devil hath no part in her. She is the Lord's, and the Lord will preserve His own."

"Will He give her back to me? Will He deliver her from the hands of His enemies?"

"The Lord is mighty even to do this. But I say not that it will be done as thou desirest. Put thy trust in Him. Did Abraham withhold his son, his only son, when God demanded him?"

"But this is not God, it is Nemausus."

"Nemausus is naught but a creature, a fountain, fed by God's rains. It is the Lord's doing that the lot has fallen thus. It is done to try thy faith, as of old the faith of Abraham was tried."

The poor mother clasped her arms, and buried her head in them.

Then the girl thrust aside such as interposed and essayed to reach her mother. The priestesses laid hands on her, to stay her, but she said:

"Suffer me to kiss my mother, and to comfort her. Do not doubt that I will preserve a smiling countenance."

"I cannot permit it," said the high priestess. "There will be resistance and tears."

"And therefore," said the girl, "you put drops of oil or water into the ears of oxen brought to the altars, that they may nod their heads, and so seem to express consent. Let me console my mother, so shall I be able to go gladly to death. Otherwise I may weep, and thereby mar thy sacrifice."

Then, with firmness, she thrust through the belt of priestesses, and clasped the almost fainting and despairing mother to her heart.

"Be of good courage," she said. "Be like unto Felicitas, who sent her sons, one by one, to receive the crown, and who—blessed mother that she was—

encouraged them in their torments to play the man for Christ."

"But thou art my only child."

"And she offered them all to God."

"I am a widow, and alone."

"And such was she."

Then said the brown-habited man whom the lady had called Baudillas:

"Quincta, remember that she is taken from an evil world, in which are snares, and that God may have chosen to deliver her by this means from some great peril to her soul, against which thou wouldst have been powerless to protect her."

"I cannot bear it," gasped the heart-broken woman. "I have lived only for her. She is my all."

Then Perpetua gently unclasped the arms of her mother, who was lapsing into unconsciousness, kissed her, and said:

"The God of all strength and comfort be to thee a strong tower of defence." And hastily returned to the basin.

The young man who before had noticed Perpetua, turned with quivering lip to his companion, and said:

"I would forswear Nemausus—that he should exact such a price. Look at her face, Callipodius. Is it the sun that lightens it? By Hercules, I could swear that it streamed with effulgence from within —as though she were one of the gods."

"The more beautiful and innocent she be, the more grateful is she to the august Archegos!"

"Pshaw!" scoffed the young man; his hand clutched the marble balustrade convulsively, and the blood suffused his brow and cheeks and throat. "I believe naught concerning these deities. My father was a shrewd man, and he ever said that the ignorant people created their own gods out of heroes, or the things of Nature, which they understood not, being beasts."

"But tell me, Æmilius—and thou art a profundity of wisdom, unsounded as is this spring—what is this Nemausus?"

"The fountain."

"And how comes the fountain to ever heave with water, and never to fail. Verily it lives. See—it is as a thing that hath life and movement. If not a deity, then what is it?"

"Nay—I cannot say. But it is subject to destiny."

"In what way?"

"Ruled to flow."

"But who imposed the rule?"

"Silence! I can think of naught save the innocent virgin thus sacrificed to besotted ignorance."

"Thou canst not prevent it. Therefore look on, as at a show."

"I cannot prevent it. I marvel at the magistrates—that they endure it. They would not do so were it to touch at all those of the upper town. Besides, did not the god Claudius——"

"They are binding her."

"She refuses to be bound."

Shrieks now rang from the frantic mother, and she made desperate efforts to reach her daughter. She was deaf to the consolations of Baudillas, and to the remonstrances and entreaties of the people around her, who pitied and yet could not help her. Then said the ædile to his police, "Remove the woman!"

The chief priest made a sign, and at once the trumpeters began to bray through their brazen tubes, making such a noise as to drown the cries of the mother.

"I would to the gods I could save her," said

Æmilius between his teeth. He clenched his hands, and his eyes flashed. Then, without well knowing what he did, he unloosed his toga, at the same time that the priestesses divested Perpetua of her girded stole, and revealed her graceful young form in the tunic bordered with purple indicative of the nobility of the house to which she belonged.

The priest had bound her hands; but Perpetua smiled, and shook off the bonds at her feet. "Let be," she said, "I shall not resist."

On her head she still wore a crown of white narcissus. Not more fresh and pure were these flowers than her delicate face, which the blood had left. Ever and anon she turned her eyes in the direction of her mother, but she could no longer see her, as the attendants formed a ring so compact that none could break through.

"Elect of the god, bride of Nemausus!" said the chief priestess, "ascend the balustrade of the holy perennial fountain."

Without shrinking, the girl obeyed.

She fixed her eyes steadily on the sky, and then made the sacred sign on her brow.

"What doest thou?" asked the priestess. "Some witchcraft I trow."

"No witchcraft, indeed," answered the girl. "I do but invoke the Father of Lights with whom is no variableness, neither shadow of turning."

"Ah, Apollo!—he is not so great a god as our Nemausus."

Then at a sign, the trumpeters blew a furious bellow and as suddenly ceased. Whereupon to the strains of flutes and the tinkling of triangles, the choir broke forth into the last verse of the hymn:

"Thou, the perennial, loving tender virgins,
　Do thou accept the sacrifice we offer ;
　May thy selection be the best and fittest,
　　Father Nemausus."

As they chanted, and a cloud of incense mounted around her, Perpetua looked down into the water. It was green as glacier ice, and so full of bubbles in places as to be there semi-opaque. The depth seemed infinite. No bottom was visible. No fish darted through it. An immense volume boiled up unceasingly from unknown, unfathomed depths. The wavelets lapped the marble breasting as though licking it with greed expecting their victim.

The water, after brimming the basin, flowed away over a sluice under a bridge as a considerable stream.

Then it lost its sanctity and was employed for profane uses.

Perpetua heard the song of the ministers of the god, but gave no heed to it, for her lips moved in prayer, and her soul was already unfurling its pure wings to soar into that Presence before which, as she surely expected, she was about to appear.

When the chorus had reached the line:

> "May thy selection be the best and fittest,
> Father Nemausus!"

then she was thrust by three priestesses from the balustrade and precipitated into the basin. She uttered no cry, but from all present a gasp of breath was audible.

For a moment she disappeared in the vitreous waters, and her white garland alone remained floating on the surface.

Then her dress glimmered, next her arm, as the surging spring threw her up.

Suddenly from the entire concourse rose a cry of astonishment and dismay.

The young man, Æmilius Lentulus Varo, had leaped into the holy basin.

Why had he so leaped? Why?

CHAPTER III

BAUDILLAS, THE DEACON

The chain of priests and priestesses could not restrain the mob, that thrust forward to the great basin, to see the result.

Exclamations of every description rose from the throng.

"He fell in!"

"Nay, he cast himself in. The god will withdraw the holy waters. It was impious. The fountain is polluted."

"Was it not defiled when a dead tom-cat was found in it? Yet the fountain ceased not to flow."

"The maiden floats!"

"Why should the god pick out the handsomest girl? His blood is ice-cold. She is not a morsel for him," scoffed a red-faced senator.

"He rises! He is swimming."

"He has grappled the damsel."

"He is striking out! Bene! Bene!"

"Encourage not the sacrilegious one! Thou makest thyself partaker in his impiety!"

"What will the magistrates do?"

"Do! Coil up like wood-lice, and uncurl only when all is forgotten."

"He is a Christian."

"His father was a philosopher. He swears by the gods."

"He is an atheist."

"See! See! He is sustaining her head."

"She is not dead; she gasps."

"Body of Bacchus! how the water boils. The god is wroth."

"Bah! It boils no more now than it did yesterday."

In the ice-green water could be seen the young man with nervous arms striking out. He held up the girl with one arm. The swell of the rising volumes of water greatly facilitated his efforts. Indeed the upsurging flood had such force, that to die by drowning in it was a death by inches, for as often as a body went beneath the surface, it was again propelled upwards.

In a minute he was at the breastwork, had one hand on it, then called: "Help, some one, to lift her out!"

Thereupon the man clothed in brown wool put

down his arms, clasped the half-conscious girl and raised her from the water. Callipodius assisted, and between them she was lifted out of the basin. The priests and priestesses remonstrated with loud cries. But some of the spectators cheered. A considerable portion of the men ranged themselves beside the two who had the girl in their arms, and prevented the ministers of Nemausus from recovering Perpetua from the hands of her rescuers.

The men of the upper town—Greek colonists, or their descendants—looked superciliously and incredulously on the cult of the Gallic deity of the fountain. It was tolerated, but laughed at, as something that belonged to a class of citizens that was below them in standing.

In another moment Æmilius Lentulus had thrown himself upon the balustrade, and stood facing the crowd, dripping from every limb, but with a laughing countenance.

Seeing that the mob was swayed by differing currents of feeling and opinion, knowing the people with whom he had to do, he stooped, whispered something into the ear of Callipodius; then, folding his arms, he looked smilingly around at the tossing crowd, and no sooner did he see his opportunity than, unclasping his arms, he assumed the attitude of an orator, and cried:

"Men and brethren of the good city of Nemausus! I marvel at ye, that ye dare to set at naught the laws of imperial and eternal Rome. Are ye not aware that the god Claudius issued an edict with special application to Gaul, that forever forbade human sacrifices? Has that edict been withdrawn? I have myself seen and read it graven in brass on the steps of the Capitoline Hill at Rome. So long as that law stands unrepealed ye are transgressors."

"The edict has fallen into desuetude, and desuetude abrogates a law!" called one man.

"Is it so? How many have suffered under Nero, under Caius, because they transgressed laws long forgotten? Let some one inform against the priesthood of Nemausus and carry the case to Rome."

A stillness fell on the assembly. The priests looked at one another.

"But see!" continued Æmilius, "I call you to witness this day. The god himself rejects such illegal offerings. Did you not perceive how he spurned the virgin from him when ye did impiously cast her into his holy urn? Does he not sustain life with his waters, and not destroy it? Had he desired the sacrifice then would he have gulped it down, and you would have seen the maiden no more. Not so! He rejected her; with his watery arms he repelled her. Every crystal wave he cast up was a rejection. I saw it, and I leaped in to deliver the god from the mortal flesh that he refused. I appeal to you all again. To whom did the silver image cast the apple? Was it to the maiden destined to die? Nay, verily, it was to her who was to live. The golden pippin was a fruit of life, whereby he designated such as he willed to live. Therefore, I say that the god loveth life and not death. Friends and citizens of Nemausus, ye have transgressed the law, and ye have violated the will of the divine Archegos who founded our city and by whose largess of water we live."

Then one in the crowd shouted: "There is a virgin cast yearly from the bridge over the Rhodanus at Avenio."

"Aye! and much doth that advantage the bridge and the city. Did not the floods last November carry away an arch and inundate an entire quarter of the town? Was the divine river forgetful that he had received his obligation, or was he ungrateful for the favor? Naught that is godlike can be either."

"He demanded another life."

"Nay! He was indignant that the fools of Avenio should continue to treat him as though he were a wild beast that had to be glutted, and not as a god. All you parents that fear for your children! Some of you have already lost your daughters, and have trembled for them; combine, and with one voice proclaim that you will no more suffer this. Look to the urn of the divine Nemausus. See how evenly the ripples run. Dip your fingers in the water and feel how passionless it is. Has he blown forth a blast of seething water and steam like the hot springs of Aquæ Sextiæ? Has his fountain clouded with anger? Was the god powerless to avenge the act when I plunged in? If he had desired the death of the maiden would he have suffered me, a mortal, to pluck her from his gelid lips? Make room on Olympus, O ye gods, and prepare a throne for Common Sense, and let her have domain over the minds of men."

"There is no such god," called one in the crowd.

"Ye know her not, so besotted are ye."

"He blasphemes, he mocks the holy and immortal ones."

"It is ye who mock them when ye make of them as great clowns as yourselves. The true eternal gods laugh to hear me speak the truth. Look at the sun. Look at the water, with its many twinkling smiles. The gods approve."

Whilst the young man thus harangued and amused the populace, Baudillas and Quincta, assisted by two female slaves of the latter, removed the drenched, dripping, and half-drowned girl. They bore her with the utmost dispatch out of the crowd down a sidewalk of the city gardens to a bench, on which they laid her, till she had sufficiently recovered to open her eyes and recognize those who surrounded her.

Then said the widow to one of the servants: "Run, Petronella, and bid the steward send porters with a litter. We must convey Perpetua as speedily as possible from hence, lest there be a riot, and the ministers of the devil stir up the people to insist upon again casting her into the water."

"By your leave, lady," said Baudillas, "I would advise that, at first, she should not be conveyed to your house, but to mine. It is probable, should that happen which you fear, that the populace may make a rush to your dwelling, in their attempt to get hold of the lady, your daughter. It were well that she remained for a while concealed in my house. Send for the porters to bring the litter later, when falls the night."

"You are right," said Quincta. "It shall be so."

"As in the Acts of the Blessed Apostles it is related that the craftsmen who lived by making silver shrines for Diana stirred up the people of Ephesus, so may it be now. There are many who get their living by the old religion, many whose position and influence depend on its maintenance, and such will not lightly allow a slight to be cast on their superstitions like as has been offered this day. But by evenfall we shall know the humor of the people. Young lady, lean on my arm and let me conduct thee to my lodging. Thou canst there abide till it is safe for thee to depart."

Then the brown-habited man took the maiden's arm.

Baudillas was a deacon of the Church in Nemausus—a man somewhat advanced in life. His humility, and, perhaps, also his lack of scholarship, prevented his aspiring to a higher office; moreover, he was an admirable minister of the Church as deacon, at a period when the office was mainly one of keeping the registers of the sick and poor, and of distributing alms among such as were in need.

The deacon was the treasurer of the Church, and he was a man selected for his business habits and practical turn of mind. By his office he was more concerned with the material than the spiritual distresses of men. Nevertheless, he was of the utmost value to the bishops and presbyters, for he was their feeler, groping among the poorest, entering into the worst haunts of misery and vice, quick to detect tokens of desire for better things, and ready to make use of every opening for giving rudimentary instruction.

Those who occupied the higher grades in the Church, even at this early period, were, for the most part, selected from the cultured and noble classes; not that the Church had respect of persons, but because of the need there was of possessing men who could penetrate into the best houses, and who, being related to the governing classes, might influence the upper strata of society, as well as that which was below. The great houses with their families of slaves in the city, and of servile laborers on their estates, possessed vast influence for good or evil. A believing master could flood a whole population that depended on him with light, and was certain to treat his slaves with Christian humanity. On the other hand, it occasionally happened that it was through a poor slave that the truth reached the heart of a master or mistress.

Baudillas led the girl, now shivering with cold, from the garden, and speedily reached a narrow street. Here the houses on each side were lofty, unadorned, and had windows only in the upper stories, arched with brick and unglazed. In cold weather they were closed with shutters.

The pavement of the street was of cobble-stones and rough. No one was visible; no sound issued from the houses, save only from one whence came the rattle of a loom; and a dog chained at a door barked furiously as the little party went by.

"This is the house," said Baudillas, and he struck against a door.

After some waiting a bar was withdrawn within, and the door, that consisted of two valves, was opened by an old, slightly lame slave.

"Pedo," said the deacon, "has all been well?"

"All is well, master," answered the man.

"Enter, ladies," said Baudillas. "My house is humble and out of repair, but it was once notable. Enter and rest you awhile. I will bid Pedo search for a change of garments for Perpetua."

"Hark," exclaimed Quincta, "I hear a sound like the roar of the sea."

"It is the voice of the people. It is a roar like that for blood, that goes up from the amphitheater."

CHAPTER IV

THE UTRICULARES

The singular transformation that had taken place in the presiding deity of the fountain, from being a nymph into a male god, had not been sufficiently complete to alter the worship of the deity. As in the days of Druidism, the sacred source was under the charge of priestesses, and although, with the change of sex of the deity, priests had been appointed to the temple, yet they were few, and occupied a position of subordination to the chief priestess. She was a woman of sagacity and knowledge of human nature. She perceived immediately how critical was the situation. If Æmilius Lentulus were allowed to proceed with his speech he would draw to him the excitable Southern minds, and it was quite possible might provoke a tumult in which the temple would be wrecked. At the least, his words would serve to chill popular devotion.

The period when Christianity began to radiate through the Roman world was one when the traditional paganism with its associated rights, that had contented a simpler age, had lost its hold on the thoughtful and cultured. Those who were esteemed the leaders of society mocked at religion, and although they conformed to its ceremonial, did so with ill-disguised contempt. At their tables, before their slaves, they laughed at the sacred myths related of the gods, as absurd and indecent, and the slaves thought it became them to affect the same incredulity as their masters. Sober thinkers endeavored to save some form of religion by explaining away the monstrous legends, and attributing them to the wayward imagination of poets. The existence of the gods they admitted, but argued that the gods were the unintelligent and blind forces of nature; or that, if rational, they stood apart in cold exclusiveness and cared naught for mankind. Many threw themselves into a position of agnosticism. They professed to believe in nothing but what their senses assured them did exist, and asserted that as there was no evidence to warrant them in declaring that there were gods, they could not believe in them; that moreover, as there was no revelation of a moral law, there existed no distinction between right and wrong. Therefore, the only workable maxim on which to rule life was: "Let us eat and drink, for to-morrow we may die."

Over all men hung the threatening cloud of death. All must undergo the waning of the vital powers, the failure of health, the withering of beauty, the loss of appetite for the pleasure of life, or if not the loss of appetite, at least the faculty for enjoyment.

There was no shaking off the oppressive burden, no escape from the gathering shadow. Yet, just as those on the edge of a precipice throw themselves over, through giddiness, so did men rush on self-destruction in startling numbers and with levity, because weary of life, and these were precisely such as had enjoyed wealth to the full and had run through the whole gamut of pleasures.

What happened after death? Was there any continuance of existence?

Men craved to know. They felt that life was too brief altogether for the satisfaction of the aspirations of their souls. They ran from one pleasure to another without filling the void within.

Consequently, having lost faith in the traditional religion—it was not a creed—itself a composite out of some Latin, some Etruscan, and some Greek myth and cult, they looked elsewhere for what they required. Consciences, agonized by remorse, sought expiation in secret mysteries, only to find that they afforded no relief at all. Minds craving after faith plunged into philosophic speculations that led to nothing but unsolved eternal query. Souls hungering, thirsting after God the Ideal of all that is Holy and pure and lovable, adopted the strange religions imported from the East and South; some became votaries of the Egyptian Isis and Serapis, others of the Persian Mithras—all to find that they had pursued bubbles.

In the midst of this general disturbance of old ideas, in the midst of a widespread despair, Christianity flashed forth and offered what was desired by the earnest, the thoughtful, the down-trodden and the conscience-stricken—a revelation made by the Father of Spirits as to what is the destiny of man, what is the law of right and wrong, what is in store for those who obey the law; how also pardon might be obtained for transgression, and grace to restore fallen humanity.

Christianity meeting a wide-felt want spread rapidly, not only among the poor and oppressed, but extensively among the cultured and the noble. All connected by interest, or prejudiced by association with the dominant and established paganism, were uneasy and alarmed. The traditional religion was honeycombed and tottering to its fall, and how it was to be revived they knew not. That it would be supplanted by the new faith in Christ was what they feared.

The chief priestess of Nemausus knew that in the then condition of minds an act of overt defiance might lead to a very general apostasy. It was to her of sovereign importance to arrest the movement at once, to silence Æmilius, to have him punished for his act of sacrilege, and to recover possession of Perpetua.

She snatched the golden apple from the hand of the image, and, giving it to an attendant, said: " Run everywhere; touch and summon the Cultores Nemausi."

The girl did as commanded. She sped among the crowd, and, with the pippin, touched one, then another, calling: " Worshippers of Nemausus, to the aid of the god! "

The result was manifest at once. It was as though an electrical shock had passed through the multitude. Those touched and those who had heard the summons at once disengaged themselves from the crush, drew together, and ceased to express their individual opinions. Indeed, such as had previously applauded the sentiments of Æmilius, now assumed an attitude of disapprobation.

Rapidly men rallied about the white-robed priestesses, who surrounded the silver image.

To understand what was taking place it is necessary that a few words should be given in explanation.

The Roman population of the towns—not in Italy only, but in all the Romanized provinces, banded itself in colleges or societies very much like our benefit clubs. Those guilds were very generally under the invocation of some god or goddess, and those who belonged to them were entitled "Cultores" or worshippers of such or such a deity. These clubs had their secretaries and treasurers, their places of meeting, their common chests, their feasts, and their several constitutions. Each society made provision for its members in time of sickness, and furnished a dignified funeral in the club Columbarium, after which all sat down to a funeral banquet in the supper room attached to the cemetery. These colleges or guilds enjoyed great privileges, and were protected by the law.

At a time when a political career was closed

to all but such as belonged to the governing class, the affairs of these clubs engrossed the attention of the members and evoked great rivalry and controversies. One admirable effect of the clubs was the development of a spirit of fellowship among the members, and another was that it tended in a measure to break down class exclusiveness. Men of rank and wealth, aware of the power exercised by these guilds, eagerly accepted the offices of patron to them, though the clubs might be those of cord-wainers, armorers or sailmakers. And those who were ordinary members of a guild regarded their patrons with affection and loyalty. Now that the signal had been sent round to rally the Cultores Nemausi, every member forgot his private feeling, sank his individual opinion, and fell into rank with his fellows, united in one common object—the maintenance by every available man, and at every sacrifice, of the respect due to the god.

These Cultores Nemausi at once formed into organized bodies under their several officers, in face of a confused crowd that drifted hither and thither without purpose and without cohesion.

Æmilius found himself no longer hearkened to. To him this was a matter of no concern. He had sought to engage attention only so as to withdraw it from Perpetua and leave opportunity for her friends to remove her.

Now that this object was attained, he laughingly leaped from the balustrade and made as though he was about to return home.

But at once the chief priestess saw his object, and cried: "Seize him! He blasphemes the god, founder of the city. He would destroy the college. Let him be conveyed into the temple, that the Holy One may there deal with him as he wills."

The Prefect of Police, whose duty it was to keep order, now advanced with the few men he had deemed necessary to bring with him, and he said in peremptory tone:

"We can suffer no violence. If he has transgressed the law, let him be impeached."

"Sir," answered the priestess, "we will use no violence. He has insulted the majesty of the god. He has snatched from him his destined and devoted victim. Yet we meditate no severe reprisals. All I seek is that he may be brought into the presence of the god in the adytum, where is a table spread with cakes. Let him there sprinkle incense on the fire and eat of the cakes. Then he shall go free.

If the god be wroth, he will manifest his indignation. But if, as I doubt not, he be placable, then shall this man depart unmolested."

"Against this I have naught to advance," said the prefect.

But one standing by whispered him: "Those cakes are not to be trusted. I have heard of one who ate and fell down in convulsions after eating."

"That is a matter between the god and Æmilius Varo. I have done my duty."

Then the confraternity of the Cultores Nemausi spread itself so as to encircle the place and include Æmilius, barring every passage. He might, doubtless, have escaped had he taken to his heels at the first summons of the club to congregate, but he had desired to occupy the attention of the people as long as possible, and it did not comport with his self-respect to run from danger.

Throwing over him the toga which he had cast aside when he leaped into the pond, he thrust one hand into his bosom and leisurely strode through the crowd, waving them aside with the other hand, till he stopped by the living barrier of the worshippers of Nemausus.

"You cannot pass, sir," said the captain of that

party which intercepted his exit. "The chief priestess hath ordered that thou appear before the god in his cella and then do worship and submit thyself to his will."

"And how is that will to be declared?" asked the young man, jestingly.

"Sir! thou must eat one of the dedicated placenta."

"I have heard of these same cakes and have no stomach for them."

"Nevertheless eat thou must."

"What if I will not?"

"Then constraint will be used. The prefect has given his consent. Who is to deliver thee?"

"Who! Here come my deliverers!"

A tramp of feet was audible.

Instantly Æmilius ran back to the balustrade, leaped upon it, and, waving his arm, shouted:

"To my aid, Utriculares! But use no violence."

Instantly with a shout a dense body of men that had rolled into the gardens dashed itself against the ring of Cultores Nemausi. They brandished marlin spikes and oars to which were attached inflated goatskins and bladders. These they whirled around their heads and with them they smote to the left and to the right. The distended skins clashed against such as stood in opposition, and sent them reeling backward; whereat the lusty men wielding the windbags thrust their way as a wedge through their ranks. The worshippers of Nemausus swore, screamed, remonstrated, but were unable to withstand the onslaught. They were beaten back and dispersed by the whirling bladders.

The general mob roared with laughter and cheered the boatmen who formed the attacking party. Cries of " Well done, Utriculares! That is a fine delivery, Wind-bag-men! Ha, ha! A hundred to five on the Utriculares! You are come in the nick of time, afore your patron was made to nibble the poisoned cakes."

The men armed with air-distended skins did harm to none. Their weapons were calculated to alarm and not to injure. To be banged in the face with a bladder was almost as disconcerting as to be smitten with a cudgel, but it left no bruise, it broke no bone, and the man sent staggering by a wind-bag was received in the arms of those in rear with jibe or laugh and elicited no compassion.

The Utriculares speedily reached Æmilius, gave

vent to a cheer; they lifted him on their shoulders, and, swinging the inflated skins and shouting, marched off, out of the gardens, through the Forum, down the main street of the lower town unmolested, under the conduct of Callipodius.

CHAPTER V

THE LAGOONS

The men who carried and surrounded Æmilius proceeded in rapid march, chanting a rhythmic song, through the town till they emerged on a sort of quay beside a wide-spreading shallow lagoon. Here were moored numerous rafts.

"Now, sir," said one of the men, as Æmilius leaped to the ground, "if you will take my advice, you will allow us to convey you at once to Arelate. This is hardly a safe place for you at present."

"I must thank you all, my gallant fellows, for your timely aid. But for you I should have been forced to eat of the dedicated cakes, and such as are out of favor with the god—or, rather, with the priesthood that lives by him, as cockroaches and black beetles by the baker—such are liable to get stomach aches, which same stomach aches convey into the land where are no aches and pains. I thank you all."

"Nay, sir, we did our duty. Are not you patron of the Utricularœ?"

"I am your patron assuredly, as you did me the honor to elect me. If I have lacked zeal to do you service in time past, henceforward be well assured I will devote my best energies to your cause."

"We are beholden to you, sir."

"I to you—the rather."

Perhaps the reader will desire to understand who the wind-bag men were who had hurried to the rescue of Æmilius. For the comprehension of this particular, something must be said relative to the physical character of the country.

The mighty Rhône that receives the melted snows of the southern slope of the Bernese Oberland and the northern incline of the opposed Pennine Alps receives also the drain of the western side of the Jura, as well as that of the Graian and Cottian Alps. The Durance pours in its auxiliary flood below Avignon.

After a rapid thaw of snow, or the breaking of charged rain clouds on the mountains, these rivers increase in volume, and as the banks of the Rhône below the junction of the Durance and St. Raphael are low, it overflows and spreads through the flat alluvial delta. It would be more exact to say that it was wont to overflow, rather than that it does so now. For at present, owing to the embankments thrown up and maintained at enormous cost, the Rhône can only occasionally submerge the low-lying land, whereas anciently such floods were periodical and as surely expected as those of the Nile.

The overflowing Rhône formed a vast region of lagoons that extended from Tarascon and Beaucaire to the Gulf of Lyons, and spread laterally over the Crau on one side to Nîmes on the other. Nîmes itself stood on its own river, the Vistre, but this fed marshes and " broads " that were connected with the tangle of lagoons formed by the Rhône.

Arelate, the great emporium of the trade between Gaul and Italy, occupied a rocky islet in the midst of water that extended as far as the eye could reach. This tract of submerged land was some sixty miles in breadth by forty in depth, was sown with islets of more or less elevation and extent. Some were bold, rocky eminences, others were mere rubble and sandbanks formed by the river. Arelate or Arles was accessible by vessels up and down the river or by rafts that plied the lagoons, and by the canal constructed by Marius, that traversed them from Fossoe Marino. As the canal was not deep, and as the current of the river was strong, ships were often unable to ascend to the city through these arteries, and had to discharge their merchandise on the coast upon rafts that conveyed it to the great town, and when the floods permitted, carried much to Nemausus.

As the sheets of water were in places and at periods shallow, the rafts were made buoyant, though heavily laden, by means of inflated skins and bladders placed beneath them.

As the conveyance of merchandise engaged a prodigious number of persons, the raftsmen had organized themselves into the guild of Utriculares, or Wind-bag men, and as they became not infrequently involved in contests with those whose interests they crossed, and on whose privileges they infringed, they enlisted the aid of lawyers to act as their patrons, to bully their enemies, and to fight their battles against assailants. Among the numerous classic monumental inscriptions that remain in Provence, there are many in which a man of position is proud to have it recorded that he was an honorary member of the club of the inflated-skin men.

Nemausus owed much of its prosperity to the fact that it was the trade center for wool and for skins. The Cevennes and the great limestone plateaux that abut upon them nourished countless herds of goats and flocks of sheep, and the dress of everyone at the period being of wool the demand for fleeces was great; consequently vast quantities of wool were brought from the mountains of Nîmes, whence it was floated away on rafts sustained by the skins that came from the same quarter.

The archipelago that studded the fresh-water sea was inhabited by fishermen, and these engaged in the raft-carriage. The district presented a singular contrast of high culture and barbarism. In Arles, Nîmes, Narbonne there was a Greek element. There was here and there an infusion of Phœnician blood. The main body of the people consisted of the dusky Ligurians, who had almost entirely lost their language, and had adopted that of their Gaulish conquerors, the Volex. These latter were distinguished by their fair hair, their clear complexions, their stalwart frames. Another element in the composite mass was that of the colonists. After the battle of Actium, Augustus had rewarded his Egypto-Greek auxiliaries by planting them at Nemausus, and giving them half the estates of the Gaulish nobility. To these Greeks were added Roman merchants, round-headed, matter-of-fact looking men, destitute of imagination, but full of practical sense.

These incongruous elements that in the lapse of centuries have been fused, were, at the time of this tale, fairly distinct.

"You are in the right, my friends," said Æmilius. "The kiln is heated too hot for comfort. It would roast me. I will go even to Arelate, if you will be good enough to convey me thither."

"With the greatest of pleasure, sir."

Æmilius had an office at Arles. He was a lawyer, but his headquarters were at Nemausus, to which town he belonged by birth. He represented a good family, and was descended from one of the colonists under Agrippa and Augustus. His father was dead, and though he was not wealthy, he was well off, and possessed a villa and estates on the mountain sides, at some distance from the town. In the heats of summer he retired to his villa.

On this day of March there had been a considerable gathering of raftsmen at Nemausus, who had utilized the swollen waters in the lagoons for the conveyance of merchandise.

Æmilius stepped upon a raft that seemed to be poised on bubbles, so light was it on the surface of the water, and the men at once thrust from land with their poles.

The bottom was everywhere visible, owing to the whiteness of the limestone pebbles and the sand that composed it, and through the water darted innumerable fish. The liquid element was clear. Neither the Vistre nor the stream from the fountain brought down any mud, and the turbid Rhône had deposited all its sediment before its waters reached and mingled with those that flowed from the Cebennæ. There was no perceptible current. The weeds under water were still, and the only thing in motion were the darting fish.

The raftmen were small, nimble fellows, with dark hair, dark eyes and pleasant faces. They laughed and chatted with each other over the incident of the rescue of their patron, but it was in their own dialect, unintelligible to Æmilius, to whom they spoke in broken Latin, in which were mingled Greek words.

Now and then they burst simultaneously into a wailing chant, and then interrupted their song to laugh and gesticulate and mimic those who had been knocked over by their wind-bags.

As Æmilius did not understand their conversation and their antics did not amuse him, he lay on the raft upon a wolfskin that had been spread over the timber, looking dreamily into the water and at the white golden flowers of the floating weeds through which the raft was impelled. The ripples caused by the displacement of the water caught and flashed the sun in his eyes like lightning.

His mind reverted to what had taken place, but unlike the raftmen he did not consider it from its humorous side. He wondered at himself for the active part he had taken. He wondered at himself for having acted without premeditation. Why had he interfered to save the life of a girl whom he had not known even by name? Why had he been so indiscreet as to involve himself in a quarrel with his fellow-citizens in a matter in no way concerning him? What had impelled him so rashly to bring down on himself the resentment of an influential and powerful body?

The youth of Rome and of the Romanized provinces was at the time of the empire very blasé. It enjoyed life early, and wearied rapidly of pleasure. It became skeptical as to virtue, and looked on the world of men with cynical contempt. It was selfish, sensual, cruel. But in Æmilius there was something nobler than what existed in most; the perception of what was good and true was not dead in him;

it had slept. And now the face of Perpetua looked up at him out of the water. Was it her beauty that had so attracted him as to make him for a moment mad and cast his cynicism aside, as the butterfly throws away the chrysalis from which it breaks? No, beautiful indeed she was, but there was in her face something inexpressible, undefinable, even mentally; something conceivable in a goddess, an aura from another world, an emanation from Olympus. It was nothing that was subject to the rule. It was not due to proportion; it could be seized by neither painter nor sculptor. What was it? That puzzled him. He had been fascinated, lifted out of his base and selfish self to risk his life to do a generous, a noble act. He was incapable of explaining to himself what had wrought this sudden change in him.

He thought over all that had taken place. How marvelous had been the serenity with which Perpetua had faced death! How ready she was to cast away life when life was in its prime and the world with all its pleasures was opening before her! He could not understand this. He had seen men die in the arena, but never thus. What had given the girl that look, as though a light within shone through her features? What was there in her that made him feel that to think of her, save with reverence, was to commit a sacrilege?

In the heart of Æmilius there was, though he knew it not, something of that same spirit which pervaded the best of men and the deepest thinkers in that decaying, corrupt old world. All had acquired a disbelief in virtue because they nowhere encountered it, and yet all were animated with a passionate longing for it as the ideal, perhaps the unattainable, but that which alone could make life really happy.

It was this which disturbed the dainty epicureanism of Horace, which gave verjuice to the cynicism of Juvenal, which roused the savage bitterness of Perseus. More markedly still, the craving after this better life, on what based, he could not conjecture, filled the pastoral mind of Virgil, and almost with a prophet's fire, certainly with an aching desire, he sang of the coming time when the vestiges of ancient fraud would be swept away and the light of a better day, a day of truth and goodness would break on the tear- and blood-stained world.

And now this dim groping after what was better than he had seen; this inarticulate yearning after something higher than the sordid round of pleasure;

this innate assurance that to man there is an ideal of spiritual loveliness and perfection to which he can attain if shown the way—all this now had found expression in the almost involuntary plunge into the Nemauscan pool. He had seen the ideal, and he had broken with the regnant paganism to reach and rescue it.

"What, my Æmilius! like Narcissus adoring thine incomparable self in the water!"

The young lawyer started, and an expression of annoyance swept over his face. The voice was that of Callipodius.

"Oh, my good friend," answered Æmilius, "I was otherwise engaged with my thoughts than in thinking of my poor self."

"Poor! with so many hides of land, vineyards and sheep-walks and olive groves! Aye, and with a flourishing business, and the possession of a matchless country residence at Ad Fines."

"Callipodius," said the patron, "thou art a worthy creature, and lackest but one thing to make thee excellent."

"And what is that?"

"Bread made without salt is insipid, and conversation seasoned with flattery nauseates. I have heard of a slave who was smeared with honey and exposed on a cross to wasps. When thou addressest me I seem to feel as though thou wast dabbing honey over me."

"My Æmilius! But where would you find wasps to sting you?"

"Oh! they are ready and eager—and I am flying them—all the votaries of Nemausus thou hast seen this day. As thou lovest me, leave me to myself, to rest. I am heavy with sleep, and the sun is hot."

"Ah! dreamer that thou art. I know that thou art thinking of the fair Perpetua, that worshiper of an——"

"Cease; I will not hear this." Æmilius made an angry gesture. Then he started up and struck at his brow. "By Hercules! I am a coward, flying, flying, when she is in extreme peril. Where is she now? Maybe those savages, those fools, are hunting after her to cast her again into the basin, or to thrust poisoned cakes into her mouth. By the Sacred Twins! I am doing that which is unworthy of me— that for which I could never condone. I am leaving the feeble and the helpless, unassisted, unprotected in extremity of danger. Thrust back, my good men! Thrust back! I cannot to Arelate. I must again to Nemausus!"

CHAPTER VI

THE PASSAGE INTO LIFE

Æmilius had sprung to his feet and called to the men to cease punting. They rested on their poles, awaiting further instructions, and the impetus given to the raft carried it among some yellow flags and rushes.

Callipodius said: "I mostly admire the splendor of your intellect, that shines forth with solar effulgence. But there are seasons when the sun is eclipsed or obscured, and such is this with thee. Surely thou dost not contemplate a return to Nemausus to risk thy life without being in any way able to assist the damsel. Consider, moreover—is it worth it—for a girl?"

"Callipodius," said the young lawyer in a tone of vehemence, "I cannot fly and place myself in security and leave her exposed to the most dreadful danger. I did my work by half only. What I did was unpremeditated, but that done must be made a complete whole. When I undertake anything it is my way to carry it out to a fair issue."

"That is true enough and worthy of your excellent qualities of heart and mind. But you know nothing of this wench, and be she all that you imagine, what is a woman that for her you should jeopardize your little finger? Besides, her mother and kinsfolk will hardly desire your aid, will certainly not invoke it."

"Why not?"

Callipodius shrugged his shoulders. "You are a man of the world—a votary of pleasure, and these people are Christians. They will do their utmost for her. They hang together as a swarm of bees."

"Who and what are these people—this mother and her kinsfolk?"

"I know little about them. They occupy a house in the lower town, and that tells its own tale. They do not belong to the quality to which you belong. The girl has been reputed beautiful, and many light fellows have sought to see and have words with her. But she is so zealously guarded, and is herself so retiring and modest that they have encountered only rebuff and disappointment."

"I must return. I will know for certain that she is in safety. Methinks no sooner were they balked of me than they would direct all their efforts to secure her."

"You shall not go back to Nemausus. You would but jeopardize your own valuable life without the possibility of assisting her; nay, rather wouldst thou direct attention to her. Leave the matter with me and trust my devotion to thine interests."

"I must learn tidings of her. I shall not rest till assured that she is out of danger. By the infernal gods, Callipodius, I know not what is come upon me, but I feel that if ill befall her, I could throw myself on a sword and welcome death, life having lost to me all value."

"Then I tell thee this, most resolute of men," said Callipodius, "I will return to the town. My nothingness will pass unquestioned. Thou shalt tarry at the house of Flavillus yonder on the promontory. He is a timber merchant, and the place is clean. The woman bears a good name, and, what is better, can cook well. The house is poor and undeserving of the honor of receiving so distinguished a person as thyself; but if thou wilt condescend——"

"Enough. I will do as thou advisest. And, oh, friend, be speedy, relieve my anxiety and be true as thou dost value my esteem."

Then Æmilius signed to the raftmen to put him ashore at the landing place to the timber yard of Flavillus.

Having landed he mounted a slight ascent to a cottage that was surrounded by piles of wood—of oak, chestnut, pine and olive. Flavillus was a merchant on a small scale, but a man of energy and industry. He dealt with the natives of the Cebennæ, and bought the timber they felled, conveyed it to his stores, whence it was distributed to the towns in the neighborhood; and supplies were furnished to the shipbuilders at Arelate.

The merchant was now away, but his wife received Æmilius with deference. She had heard his name from the raftmen, and was acquainted with Callipodius, a word from whom sufficed as an introduction.

She apologized because her house was small, as also because her mother, then with her, was at the point of death from old age, not from any fever or other disorder. If Æmilius Lentulus, under the circumstances, would pardon imperfection in attendance, she would gladly extend to him such hospitality as she could offer. Æmilius would have gone elsewhere, but that the only other house he could think of that was near was a tavern, then crowded by Utriculares, who occupied every corner. He was sorry to inconvenience the woman, yet accepted her offer. The period was not one in which much consideration was shown to those in a lower grade. The citizens and nobles held that their inferiors existed for their convenience only. Æmilius shared in the ideas of his time and class, but he had sufficient natural delicacy to make him reluctant to intrude where his presence was necessarily irksome. Nevertheless, as there was no other place to which he could go, he put aside this feeling of hesitation.

The house was small, and was constructed of wood upon a stone basement. The partitions between the rooms were of split planks, and the joints were in places open, and knots had come out, so that what passed in one apartment was audible, and, to some extent, visible in another. A bedroom in a Roman house was a mere closet, furnished with a bed only. All washing was done at the baths, not in the house. The room had no window, only a door over which hung a curtain.

Æmilius divested himself of his wet garment and gave it to his hostess to dry, then wrapped himself in his toga and awaited supper.

The meal was prepared as speedily as might be.

It consisted of eggs, eels, with melon, and apples of last year. Wine was abundant, and so was oil.

When he had eaten and was refreshed, moved by a kindly thought Æmilius asked if he might see the sick mother. His hostess at once conducted him to her apartment, and he stood by the old woman's bed. The evening sun shone in at the door, where stood the daughter holding back the curtain, and lighted the face of the aged woman. It was thin, white and drawn. The eyes were large and lustrous.

"I am an intruder," said the young man, "yet I would not sleep the night in this house without paying my respects to the mother of my kind hostess. Alas! thou art one I learn who is unable to escape that which befalls all mortals. It is a lot evaded only by the gods, if there be any truth in the tales told concerning them. It must be a satisfaction to you to contemplate the many pleasures enjoyed in a long life, just as after an excellent meal we can in mind revert to it and retaste in imagination every course—as indeed I do with the supper so daintily furnished by my hostess."

"Ah, sir," said the old woman, "on the couch of death one looks not back but forward."

"And that also is true," remarked Æmilius. "What is before you but everything that can console the mind and gratify the ambition. With your excellent daughter and the timber-yard hard by, you may calculate on a really handsome funeral pyre—plenty of olive wood and fragrant pine logs from the Cebennæ. I myself will be glad to contribute a handful of oriental spices to throw into the flames."

"Sir, I think not of that."

"And the numbers who will attend and the orations that will be made lauding your many virtues! It has struck me that one thing only is wanting in a funeral to make it perfectly satisfactory, and that is that the person consigned to the flames should be able to see the pomp and hear the good things said of him."

"Oh, sir, I regard not that!"

"No, like a wise woman, you look beyond."

"Aye! aye!" she folded her hands and a light came into her eyes. "I look beyond."

"To the mausoleum and the cenotaph. Unquestionably the worthy Flavillus will give you a monument as handsome as his means will permit, and for many centuries your name will be memorialized thereon."

"Oh, sir! my poor name! what care I for that? I ask Flavillus to spend no money over my remains; and may my name be enshrined in the heart of my daughter. But—it is written elsewhere—even in Heaven."

"I hardly comprehend."

"As to what happens to the body—that is of little concern to me. I desire but one thing—to be dissolved, and to be with Christ."

"Ah!—so—with Christ!"

Æmilius rubbed his chin.

"He is my Hope. He is my Salvation. In Him I shall live. Death is swallowed up in Victory."

"She rambles in her talk," said he, turning to the daughter.

"Nay, sir, she is clear in her mind and dwells on the thoughts that comfort her."

"And that is not that she will have an expensive funeral?"

"Oh, no, sir!"

"Nor that she will have a commemorative cenotaph belauding her virtues?"

Then the dying woman said: "I shall live—live forevermore. I have passed from death unto life."

Æmilius shook his head. If this was not the raving of a disordered mind, what could it be?

He retired to his apartment.

He was tired. He had nothing to occupy him, so he cast himself on his bed.

Shortly he heard the voice of a man. He started and listened in the hopes that Callipodius had returned, but as the tones were strange to him he lay down again.

Presently a light struck through a knot in the boards that divided his room from that of the dying woman. Then he heard the strange voice say: "Peace be to this house and to all that dwell therein."

"It is the physician," said Æmilius to himself. "Pshaw! what can he do? She is dying of old age."

At first the newcomer did inquire concerning the health of the patient, but then rapidly passed to other matters, and these strange to the ear of the young lawyer. He had gathered that the old woman was a Christian; but of Christians he knew no more than that they were reported to worship the head of an ass, to devour little children, and to indulge in debauchery at their evening banquets.

The strange man spoke to the dying woman—not of funeral and cenotaph as things to look forward to, but to life and immortality, to joy and rest from labor.

"My daughter," said the stranger, "indicate by sign that thou hearest me. Fortified by the most precious gift thou wilt pass out of darkness into light, out of sorrow into joy, from tears to gladness of heart, from where thou seest through a glass darkly to where thou shalt look on the face of Christ, the Sun of Righteousness. Though thou steppest down into the river, yet His cross shall be thy stay and His staff shall comfort thee. He goeth before to be thy guide. He standeth to be thy defence. The spirits of evil cannot hurt thee. The Good Shepherd will gather thee into His fold. The True Physician will heal all thine infirmities. As the second Joshua, He will lead thee out of the wilderness into the land of Promise. The angels of God surround thee. The light of the heavenly city streams over thee. Rejoice, rejoice! The night is done and the day is at hand. For all thy labors thou shalt be recompensed double. For all thy sorrows He will comfort thee. He will wipe away thy tears. He will cleanse thee from thy stains.

He will feed thee with all thy desire. Old things are passed away; all things are made new. Thy heart shall laugh and sing—Pax!"

Æmilius, looking through a chink, saw the stranger lay his hand on the woman's brow. He saw how the next moment he withdrew it, and how, turning to her daughter, he said:

"Do not lament for her. She has passed from death unto life. She sees Him, in whom she has believed, in whom she has hoped, whom she has loved."

And the daughter wiped her eyes.

"Well," said Æmilius to himself, "now I begin to see how these people are led to face death without fear. It is a pity that it should be delusion and mere talk. Where is the evidence that it is other? Where is the foundation for all this that is said?"

CHAPTER VII

OBLATIONS

The house into which the widow lady and her daughter entered was that used by the Christians of Nemausus as their church. A passage led into the *atrium*, a quadrangular court in the midst of the house into which most of the rooms opened, and in the center of which was a small basin of water. On the marble breasting of this tank stood, in a heathen household, the altar to the *lares et penates*, the tutelary gods of the dwelling. This court was open above for the admission of light and air, and to allow the smoke to escape. Originally this had been the central chamber of the Roman house, but eventually it became a court. It was the focus of family life, and the altar in it represented the primitive family hearth in times before civilization had developed the house out of the cabin.

Whoever entered a pagan household was expected, as token of respect, to strew a few grains of incense on the ever-burning hearth, or to dip his fingers in the water basin and flip a few drops over the images. But in a Christian household no such altar and images of gods were to be found. A Christian gave great offense by refusing to comply with the generally received customs, and his disregard on this point of etiquette was held to be as indicative of boorishness and lack of graceful courtesy, as would be the conduct nowadays of a man who walked into a drawing-room wearing his hat.

Immediately opposite the entrance into the *atrium*, on the further side of the tank, and beyond the altar to the *lares et penates*, elevated above the floor of the court by two or three white-marble steps, was a semicircular chamber, with elaborate mosaic floor, and the walls richly painted. This was the *tablinum*. The paintings represented scenes from heathen mythology in such houses as belonged to pagans, but in the dwelling of Baudillas, the deacon, the pictures that had originally decorated it had been plastered over, and upon this coating green vines had been somewhat rudely drawn, with birds of various descriptions playing among the foliage and pecking at the grapes.

Around the wall were seats; and here, in a pagan house, the master received his guests. His seat was at the extremity of the apse, and was of white marble. When such a house was employed for Christian worship, the clergy occupied the seat against the wall and the bishop that of the master in the center. In the chord of the apse above the steps stood the altar, now no longer smoking nor dedicated to the *Lar pater*, but devoted to Him who is the Father of Spirits. But this altar was in itself different wholly from that which had stood by the water tank. Instead of being a block of marble, with a hearth on top, it consisted of a table on three, sometimes four, bronze legs, the slab sometimes of stone, more generally of wood.*

The *tablinum* was shut off from the hall or court, except when used for the reception of guests, by rich curtains running on rings upon a rod. These curtains were drawn back or forward during the celebration of the liturgy, and this has continued to form a portion of the furniture of an Oriental church, whether Greek, Armenian, or Syrian.

In like manner the *tablinum*, with its conch-shape termination, gave the type to the absidal chancel, so general everywhere except in England.

---

* So represented in paintings in the Catacombs. There were two distinct types: the table in the Church and the tomb at the Sepulcher of the Martyr.

On the right side of the court was the *triclinium* or dining-room, and this was employed by the early Christians for their love-feasts.

Owing to the protection extended by law to the colleges or clubs, the Christians sought to screen themselves from persecution by representing themselves as forming one of these clubs, and affecting their usages. Even on their tombstones they so designated themselves, " Cultores Dei," and they were able to carry on their worship under the appearance of frequenting guild meetings. One of the notable features of such secular or semi-religious societies was the convivial supper for the members, attended by all. The Church adopted this supper, called it Agape, but of course gave to it a special signification. It was made to be a symbol of that unity among Christians which was supposed to exist between all members. The supper was also a convenient means whereby the rich could contribute to the necessities of the poor, and was regarded as a fulfilment of the Lord's command: " When thou makest a feast, call the poor, the maimed, the lame, the blind."

Already, in the third century, the believers who belonged to the superior classes had withdrawn from them, and alleged as their excuse the command: "When thou makest a dinner or a supper, call not thy friends, nor thy brethren, neither thy kinsman, nor thy rich neighbors." Their actual reason was, however, distaste for associating with such as belonged to the lower orders, and from being present at scenes that were not always edifying.

The house of Baudillas had once been of consequence, and his family one of position; but that had been in the early days of the colony before the indigenous Gaulish nobility had been ousted from every place of authority, and the means for enriching themselves had been drawn away by the greed of the conquerors. The quarter of the town in which was his mansion had declined in respectability. Many of the houses of the old Volcian gentry had been sold and converted into lodgings for artisans. In this case the ancestral dwelling remained in the possession of the last representative of the family, but it was out of repair, and the owner was poor.

"I hardly know what should be done," said Baudillas to himself, rather than to the ladies he was escorting. "The Church has been enjoined to assemble this afternoon for the Agape, and our bishop,

Castor, is absent at this critical juncture. He has gone on a pastoral round, taking advantage of the floods to visit, in boat, some of the outlying hamlets and villages where there are believers. It seems to me hardly prudent for us to assemble when there is such agitation of spirits. Ladies, allow my house-keeper—she was my nurse—to conduct you where you can repose after the fatigue and distress you have undergone. She will provide dry garments for Perpetua, and hot water for her feet. The baths are the proper place, but it would be dangerous for her to adventure herself in public."

Baudillas paced the court in anxiety of mind. He did not know what course to adopt. He was not a man of initiative. He was devoted to his duty and discharged whatever he was commanded to do with punctilious nicety; but he was thrown into helpless incapacity when undirected by a superior mind, or not controlled by a dominant will.

It would be difficult to communicate with the brethren. He had but one male servant, Pedo, who had a stiff hip-joint. He could not send him round to give notice of a postponement, and Baudillas was not the man to take such a step without orders. Probably, said he to himself, the commotion would abate before evening. There would be much feasting in the town that afternoon. The Cultores Nemausi had their club dinner; and the families of Volcian descent made it a point of honor to entertain on that day, dedicated to their Gallic founder and hero-god. It was precisely for this reason that the Agape had been appointed to be celebrated on the first of March. When all the lower town was holding debauch, the harmless reunion of the Christians would pass unregarded.

"What shall I do?" said the deacon. "Castor, our bishop, should not have absented himself at such a time, but then how could he have foreseen what has taken place? I will take care that the ladies be provided with whatever they may need, and then will sally forth and ascertain what temper our fellow-citizens are in. We southerners blaze up like a fire of straw, and as soon does our flame expire. If I meet some of the brethren, I will consult with them what is to be done. As it is we have postponed the Agape till set of sun, when we deemed that all the town would be indoors merry-making."

An hour later, a slave of the lady Quincta arrived to say that her house was watched, and that the servants did not deem it advisable to leave with the litter, lest some attempt should be made to track them to the house where their mistress was concealed, in which case the rabble might even try to get possession of Perpetua.

Quincta was greatly alarmed at the tidings, and bade that the litter should on no account be sent. When those watching her door had been withdrawn, then a faithful slave was to announce the fact, and she and her daughter would steal home afoot. Thus passed the time, with anxiety contracting the hearts of all. Quincta was a timid woman, Baudillas, as already said, irresolute. In the afternoon, gifts began to arrive for the love-feast. Slaves brought hampers of bread, quails, field-fare stuffed with truffles; brown pots containing honey were also deposited by them in the passage. Others brought branches of dried raisins, apples, eggs, flasks of oil, and bouquets of spring flowers.*

Baudillas was relieved when the stream of oblations began to flow in, as it decided for him the

---

* St. Clement of Alexandria complained of the dainties provided for the Agape: "The sauces, cakes, sugar-plums, the drink, the delicacies, the games, the sweetmeats, the honey." The hour of supper with the Romans was about 2 P.M.; that, therefore, was the time for the love-feast to begin.

matter of the Agape. It must take place—it could not be deferred, as some of the food sent was perishable.

A slave arrived laden with an *amphora*—a red earthenware bottle, pointed below, so that to maintain it upright it had to be planted in sand or ashes. On the side was a seal with the sacred symbol, showing that it contained wine set apart for religious usage.*

"Sir!" said the bearer, "happy is the man who tastes of this wine from Ambrussum (near Lunel).* It is of the color of amber, it is old, and runs like oil. The heat of the Provence sun is gathered and stored in it, to break forth and glow in the veins, to mount into and fire the brain, and to make and kindle a furnace in the heart."

"It shall be used with discretion, Tarsius," said the deacon.

"By Bacchus!—I ask your pardon, deacon! Old habits are not easily laid aside. What was I saying? Oh—you remarked something about discretion.

---

* In the recently-exhumed house of Saints John and Paul, in the Cœlian Hill at Rome, such bottles were discovered in the cellar.

† Now Ambroix.

For my part I consider that my master has exercised none in sending this to your love-feast. Bah! it is casting pearls before swine to pour out this precious essence into the cups of such a beggarly, vagabond set as assemble here. The quality folk are becoming weary of these banquets and hold aloof."

"That is sadly true," observed Baudillas, "and the effect of this withdrawal is that it aggravates the difficulties of myself and my brethren."

"The choice liquor is thrown away on such as you have as congregation. How can they relish the Ambrussian if they have not had their palates educated to know good liquor from bad? On my faith as a Christian! were I master instead of slave, I would send you the wine of the year when Sosius Falco and Julius Clarus were consuls—then the grapes mildewed in the bunch, and the wine is naught but vinegar, no color, no bouquet, no substance. Gentlemen and slaves can't drink it. But I reckon that my master thinks to condone his absence by sending one of his choicest flasks."

"You are somewhat free of tongue, Tarsius."

"I am a frank man though enslaved. Thoughts are free, and my tongue is not enchained. I shall attend the banquet this evening. The master and mistress remain at home that we, believing members of the family, may be present at the Agape. I will trouble you, when pouring out the Ambrussian wine, not to forget that I had to sweat under the flask, to your house."

"I think, Tarsius, I cannot do better than place the bottle under your charge. You know its value, and the force of the wine. Distribute as you see fit."

"Aye; I know who will appreciate it, and who are unworthy of a drop. I accept the responsibility. You do wisely, deacon, in trusting me—a knowing one," and he slapped his breast and pursed up his mouth.

Then another servant appeared with a basket.

"Here, sir!" said he to the deacon. "I bring you honey-cakes. The lady Lampridia sends them. She is infirm and unable to leave her house, but she would fain do something for the poor, the almoners of Christ. She sends you these and also garments that she has made for children. She desires that you will distribute them among such parents as have occasion for them."

Next came a man of equestrian rank, and drew the deacon aside.

"Where is Castor?" he inquired in an agitated voice. "I cannot appear this evening. The whole town is in effervescence. Inquisition may be made for us Christians. There will be a tumult. When they persecute you in one city—fly to another! That is the divine command, and I shall obey it to the letter. I have sent forward servants and mules —and shall escape with my wife and children to my villa."

"The bishop is away. He will be back this evening. I have not known what to do, whether or not to postpone the Agape to another day."

"No harm will come of it if you hold the feast. None will attend save the poor and such as are on the books of the Church, the widows and those to whom a good meal is a boon. The authorities will not trouble themselves about the like of them. I don't relish the aspect of affairs, and shall be off before the storm breaks." Then the knight added hastily, "Here is money, distribute it, and bid the recipients pray for me and mine, that no harm befall us."

Baudillas saw that the man was quaking with apprehension. "Verily," said he to himself, "It is a true saying, 'How hardly shall they that have riches enter into the kingdom of Heaven.' I wonder now, whether I have acted judiciously in entrusting that old Ambrussian to Tarsius? If the bishop had been here, I could have consulted him."

So a weak, but good man, may even do a thing fraught with greater mischief than can be done with evil intent by an adversary.

CHAPTER VIII

THE VOICE AT MIDNIGHT

As soon as dusk began to veil the sky, Christians in parties of three and four came to the house of Baudillas. They belonged for the most part to the lowest classes. None were admitted till they had given the pass-word.

An *ostiarius* or porter kept the door, and as each tapped, he said in Greek: "Beloved, let us love one another." Whereupon the applicant for admission replied in the same tongue, "For love is of God."

Owing to the Greek element in the province, large at Massilia, Arelate and Narbo, but not less considerable at Nemausus, the Hellenic tongue, though not generally spoken, was more or less comprehended by all in the towns. The Scriptures were read in Greek; there was, as yet, no Italic version, and the prayers were recited, sometimes in Greek, sometimes in Latin. In preaching, the bishops and presbyters employed the vernacular—this was a conglomerate of many tongues and was in incessant decomposition, flux, and recomposition.

It was different in every town, and varied from year to year.

In the sub-apostolic church it was customary for a banquet to be held in commemoration of the Paschal Supper, early in the afternoon, lasting all night, previous to the celebration of the new Eucharistic rite, which took place at dawn. The night was spent in hymn singing, in discourses, and in prayer.

But even in the Apostolic age, as we learn from St. Paul's first Epistle to the Corinthians, great abuses had manifested themselves, and very speedily a change was made. The Agape was dissociated from the Eucharist and was relegated to the evening after the celebration of the Sacrament. It was not abolished altogether, because it was a symbol of unity, and because, when under control, it was unobjectionable. Moreover, as already intimated, it served a convenient purpose to the Christians by making their meetings resemble those of the benefit clubs that were under legal protection.

It may be conjectured that where the bulk of the members were newly converted, and were ignorant, there would speedily manifest itself among them a tendency to revert to their pagan customs, and a revolt against the restraints of Christian sobriety.

And this actually took place, causing much embarrassment to the clergy, and giving some handle to the heathen to deride these meetings as scenes of gross disorder.

No sooner did persecution cease, and the reason for holding love-feasts no longer held, than they were everywhere put down and by the end of the fourth century had absolutely ceased.

In the third century Tertullian, in his "Apology" addressed to the heathen, gave a rose-colored description of the institution; but in his "Treatise on Fasting" addressed to the faithful, he was constrained to admit that it was a nursery of abuses. But this, indeed, common sense and a knowledge of human nature would lead us to suspect.

We are prone to imagine that the first ages of the Church saw only saints within the fold, and sinners without. But we have only to read the writings of the early Fathers to see that this was not the case. If we consider our mission stations at the present day, and consult our evangelists among the heathen, we shall discover that the newly converted on entering the Church, bring with them much of their past: their prejudices, their superstitions, their ignorance, and their passions. The most vigilant care has to be exercised in watching against relapse in the individual, and deterioration of the general tone. The converts in the first ages were not made of other flesh and blood than those now introduced into the sheepfold, and the difficulties now encountered by missionaries beset the first pastors of Christ fifteen and sixteen hundred years ago.

In an honest attempt to portray the condition of the Church at the opening of the third century, we must describe things as they were, and not as we should wish them to have been.

The *atrium* or courtyard was not lighted; there was sufficient illumination from above. The curtains of the *tablinum* were close drawn, as the reception chamber was not to be put in requisition that night. The *triclinium* or dining-room that received light through the doorway only would have been dark had not a lamp or two been kindled there.

About thirty persons were present, male and female, but no children. Some were slaves from believing households; there were a few freedmen. Some were poor artisans, weavers, bakers, and men who sold charcoal, a porter, and a besom-maker.

Quincta and Perpetua were the highest in social position of those present. A second deacon, named

Marcianus, was there, a handsome man, peremptory in manner, quick in movement; in every point a contrast with his timid, hesitating brother in the ministry.

The bishop had not arrived when the Agape began, and the blessing was spoken by an aged and feeble presbyter. The tables were spread with viands, and the deacons and deaconesses ministered to those who reclined at them. There was not room for all in the dining-chamber, and a table and couches had been spread in the court for such as could not be accommodated within.

The proceedings were marked by the strictest propriety, the eating and drinking were in moderation, conversation was edifying, and general harmony prevailed. During the meal, a knocking was heard at the outer gate, and when the porter asked the name of the applicant for admission, the password was given, and he was admitted.

All rose to receive Castor, the bishop.

"Recline again, my friends," said he. "I have come from the house of Flavillus, the timber merchant on the *stagna;* his wife's mother has endured that which is human. She sleeps, and her spirit is with the Lord. I have been delayed. I was doing the work of my Master. One, a stranger to the faith, questioned me, and I tarried to converse with him, and disclose to his dark mind some ray of light. If the supper be ended, I will offer thanks."

Then, standing at one of the tables, he made prayer to God, and thanked Him who had caused the corn to spring out of the earth, and had gathered the many grains into one bread; who had watered the vine from heaven, and had flushed the several grapes with generous juice, uniting the many into one bunch.

The thanksgiving ended, lights were introduced in considerable numbers. There is no twilight in southern climes; when night falls, it falls darkly. Now all who had eaten went to the *impluvium*, dipped their hands, and washed their lips, then wiped them on towels held by the deaconesses.

The tables were quickly removed, and the benches ranged in the *triclinium*, so as to accommodate all.

No sooner was the whole congregation assembled, than the president, Castor, invited all such as had a psalm, an interpretation, a vision, or an edifying narrative, to relate or recite it.

Then up started a little man, who held a lyre.

"Sir," said he, "I have composed a poem in honor of Andeolus, the martyr of Gentibus."

He struck a chord on his instrument, and sang. The composition was devoid of poetry, the meter halting, the Latin full of provincialisms, and the place of poetic imagery was filled with extravagances of expression. When he had concluded, he perhaps inadvertently wound up with the words, "Generous audience, grant me your applause!"—the usual method of conclusion on the stage.

And the request met with favor—hands were clapped.

Then Bishop Castor rose, and with a grave face, said:

"We have listened to Lartius Garrulus with interest and with edification. It is well to glorify the memories of the holy ones who have witnessed a good confession, who have fought the fight, and have shed their blood as a testimony. But a poet in treating of such subjects, should restrain his too exuberant fancy, and not assert as facts matters of mere conjecture, nor should he use expressions that, though perhaps endurable in poetry, cannot be addressed to the martyrs in sober prose. The ignorant are too ready to employ words without considering their meaning with nicety, and to quote poets as licensing them to do that which their pastors would forbid."

"But," said the deacon Marcianus, "what if this be uttered by inspiration?"

"The Spirit of God," answered Castor, "never inspires the mind to import into religion anything that is not true." Turning round, he said: "I call on Turgellius to interpret a portion of the Epistle of the Blessed Paul, the Apostle to the Romans, translating it into the vulgar tongue, as there be those present who comprehend Greek with difficulty."

This done, one rose, and said:

"Sir, suffer me to disclose a revelation. I was asleep on my bed, three nights agone, and I had a dream, or vision, from on high. I beheld a snow-white flock pasturing on a mountain; there was abundance of herbage, and the sky was serene. The shepherd stood regarding them, leaning on his staff, and the watch-dog slept at his feet in the grass. Then, suddenly, the heavens became obscured, lightning flashed, thunder rolled: the flock was terrified and scattered. Thereupon came wolves, leaping among the sheep, and rending them; and I beheld now that some which I had taken to be sheep, cast their skins, and disclosed themselves to be ravening beasts. What may be signified by the vision, I know not, but I greatly fear that it portends an evil time to the Church."

"That is like enough," said Baudillas, "after what has occurred this day. If the bishop has not heard, I will relate all to him in order."

"I have been informed of everything," said Castor.

"It is well that there should be a sifting of the wheat from the chaff," said Marcianus. "Too long have we had wolves masquerading among us clothed in sheepskins. See!" He threw back his mantle, and extended his hand. "On my way hither, I passed by the fountain of Nemausus, and none were there. Then my soul was wrath within me at the idolatry and worship of devils that goes on in the temple and about the basin. So I took up a stone, and I climbed upon the pedestal, and I beat till I had broken this off." Then he rolled an alabaster sculptured head on the floor. With a contemptuous kick, he sent it spinning. "This is their god Nemausus. A deacon of Christ's Church, with a bit of stone, is able to break his neck, and carry off his head!"

Then he laughed. But none laughed in response.

A thrill of dismay ran through the assembly.

A woman fell into hysterics and screamed. Some called out that she prophesied, others that she spake with tongues. Baudillas appeased the excitement. "The tongue she speaks," said he, "is the Ligurian of the Cebennæ, and all she says is that she wishes she were safe with her children in the mountains, and had never come into the town. Now, indeed, it seems that the evil days foreseen by Pantilius Narbo will come on the Church. The people might forget that the god was robbed of his victim, but not that his image has been defaced."

"Well done, I say!" shouted a man, thrusting himself forward. His face was inflamed and his eyes dazed. "I—I, Tarsius the slave, and Marcianus, the deacon, are the only Christians with any pluck about us. Cowards that ye all are, quaking at the moment of danger—hares, ye are, hares afraid of the whistling of the wind in the grass. I—I——"

"Remove that man," said the bishop. "He has been drinking."

"I—I drinking. I have supped the precious

Ambrussian wine, too good for the rag-tag. Dost think I would pour out to him who binds brooms? Or to her—a washerwoman from the mountains? Ambrussian wine for such as appreciate good things—gold as amber, thick as oil, sweet as honey."

"Remove him," said the bishop firmly.

Hands were laid on the fellow.

Then turning to Marcianus, Castor said sternly, "You have acted inconsiderately and wrongly, against the decrees of the Fathers."

"Aye!—of men who were timorous, and forbade others doing that from which they shrank themselves. I have not so learned Christ."

"Thou thyself mayest be strong," said Castor, "but thine act will bring the tempest upon the Church, and it will fall upon the weak and young."

"Such as cannot stand against the storm are good for naught," said Marcianus. "But the storm is none of my brewing. It had arisen before I intervened. The escape of the lady Perpetua from the fountain—that was the beginning, I have but added the final stroke."

"Thou hast acted very wrongly," said the bishop. "May God, the God of all comfort, strengthen us to stand in the evil day. In very truth, the powers of darkness will combine against the Church. The lightnings will indeed flash, the sheep be scattered, and those revealed whom we have esteemed to be true disciples of Christ, but who are far from Him in heart. Many that are first shall be last, and the last first. It is ever so in the Kingdom of Christ—hark!"

Suddenly a strange, a terrible sound was heard—a loud, hoarse note, like a blast blown through a triton's shell, but far louder; it seemed to pass in the air over the house, and set the tiles quivering. Every wall vibrated to it, and every heart thrilled as well. Men rushed into the *atrium* and looked up at the night sky. Stars twinkled. Nothing extraordinary was visible. But those who looked expected to see some fire-breathing monster flying athwart the dark, heavenly vault, braying; and others again cried out that this was the trumpet of the archangel, and that the end of all things was come.

Then said Marcianus, "It is the voice of the devil Nemausus! He has thus shouted before."

CHAPTER IX

STARS IN WATER

As an excuse for not appearing in time at the Agape, Castor had asserted that he had been engaged on his Master's work elsewhere. That was true. He had been at the house of the timber merchant as we have seen, and he had been detained by Æmilius as he left it. This latter had been lying on his bed resting, whilst his garments were being dried.

He had overheard what had passed in the room of the dying woman.

When the bishop went forth, then Æmilius rose from his bed, cast the ample toga about him, and walked forth. He caught Castor as he descended to the water's edge to be paddled away.

After a short salutation, the young lawyer said: "A word with you, sir, if your time is as generously to be disposed of to a stranger as it is lavished on the poor and sick."

"I am at your service," answered the bishop.

"My name," said the young man, "is Æmilius Lentulus Varo. My profession is the law. I am not, I believe, unknown in Nemausus, or at Arelate, where also I have an office. But you, sir, may not have heard of me—we have assuredly never met. Your age and gravity of demeanor belong to a social group other than mine. You mix with the wise, the philosophers, and not with such butterflies as myself, who am a ridiculous pleasure seeker— seeking and never finding. If I am not in error, you are Castor Lepidus Villoneos, of an ancient magisterial family in Nemausus and the reputed head of the Christian sect."

"I am he," answered the bishop.

"It may appear to you a piece of idle curiosity," said the young man, "if I put to you certain questions, and esteem it an impertinence, and so send me away empty. But I pray you to afford me—if thy courtesy will suffer it—some information concerning a matter on which I am eager to obtain light. I have been in the apartment adjoining that in which the mother of the hostess lay, and I chanced —the partition being but of plank—to overhear what was said. I confess that I am inquisitive to know something more certain of this philosophy or superstition, than what is commonly reported among the people. On this account, I venture to detain you, as one qualified to satisfy my greed for knowledge."

"My time is at your disposal."

"You spoke to the dying woman as though she were about to pass into a new life. Was that a poetic fancy or a philosophic speculation?"

"It was neither, it was a religious conviction. I spoke of what I knew to be true."

"Knew to be true!" laughed Æmilius. "How so? Have you traveled into the world of spirits, visited the *manes*, and returned posted up in all particulars concerning them?"

"No. I receive the testimony from One I can trust."

"One! All men are liars. I knew a fellow who related that he had fallen into an epileptic fit, and that during the fit his spirit had crossed the Styx. But as he had no penny wherewith to pay the fare, I did not believe him. Moreover, he never told the story twice alike, and in other matters was an arrant liar."

"Whom would you believe?"

"None, nothing save my own experience."

"Not Him who made and who sustains your existence, my good sir?"

"Yes, if I knew Him and were assured He spoke."

"That is the assurance I have."

Æmilius shook his head. "When, how, where, and by whom did He declare to men that there is a life beyond the tomb?"

"The *when* was in the principate of Tiberius Cæsar, the *how* was by the mouth of His only-begotten Son, the *where* was in Palestine."

The young lawyer laughed. "There is not a greater rogue and liar on the face of the earth than a Jew. I cannot believe in a revelation made elsewhere than at the center of the world, in the city of Rome."

"Rome is the center of the world to you—but is it so to the infinite God?"

Æmilius shrugged his shoulders contemptuously. "I am a lawyer. I ask for evidence. And I would not trust the word of a Jew against that of a common Gaulish peasant."

"Nor need you. The witness is in yourself."

"I do not understand you."

"Have not all men, at all times and everywhere desired to know what is to be their condition after death? Does not every barbarous people harbor the conviction that there is a future life? Do not you civilized Romans, though you have no evidence, act as though there were such a life, and testify thereto on your monumental cenotaphs?"

"I allow all that. But what of it?"

"How comes it that there should be such a conviction based on no grounds whatever, but a vague longing, unless there were such a reality provided for those who have this desire in them? Would the Creator of man mock him? Would He put this hunger into him unless it were to be satisfied? You have eyes that crave for the light, and the light exists that satisfies this longing! You have ears that desire sounds, and the world is full of voices that meet this desire. Where there is a craving there is ever a reality that corresponds with and gives repose to that desire. Look," said the bishop, and pointed to the water in which were reflected the stars that now began to glitter in the sky. "Do you see all those twinkling points in the still water? They correspond to the living luminaries set above in the vault. You in your soul have these reflections—sometimes seen, sometimes obscured, but ever returning. They answer to realities in the celestial world overhead. The reflections could not be in your nature unless they existed in substance above."

"There is a score of other things we long after in vain here."

"What things? I believe I know. Purity, perfection, justice. Well, you do not find them here entire—only in broken glints. But these glints assure you that in their integrity they do exist."

A boat was propelled through the water. It broke the reflections, that disappeared or were resolved into a very dust of sparkles. As the wavelets subsided, however, the reflections reformed.

Castor walked up and down beside Æmilius in silence for a few turns, then said:—

"The world is full of inequalities and injustices. One man suffers privation, another is gorged. One riots in luxury at the expense of the weak. Is there to be no righting of wrongs? no justice to be ever done? If there be a God over all, He must, if just—and who can conceive of God, save as perfectly just?—He must, I say, deal righteous judgment and smooth out all these creases; and how can he do so, unless there be a condition of existence after death in which the wrongs may be redressed, the evildoers be punished, and tears be wiped away?"

"There is philosophy in this."

"Have you not in your conscience a sense of right as distinct from wrong—obscured often, but ever returning—like the reflection of the stars in the water? How comes it there unless there be the verities above? Unless your Maker so made you as to reflect them in your spirit?"

Æmilius said nothing.

"Have you not in you a sense of the sacredness of Truth, and a loathing for falsehood? How comes that, unless implanted in you by your Creator, who is Truth itself?"

"But we know not—in what is of supreme interest to us—in matters connected with the gods, what our duties, what our destiny—what is the Truth."

"Young man," said the bishop, "thou art a seeker after the kingdom of Heaven. One word further, and I must leave thee. Granted there are these scintillations within——"

"Yes, I grant this."

"And that they be reflections of verities above."

"Possibly."

"Whence else come they?"

Æmilius did not, could not answer.

"Then," said Castor, "is it not antecedently probable that the God who made man, and put into his nature this desire after truth, virtue, holiness, justice, aye, and this hunger after immortality, should reveal to man that without which man is unable to direct his life aright, attain to the perfection of his being, and look beyond death with confidence?"

"If there were but such a revelation!"

"I say—is it conceivable that the Creator should not make it?"

"Thou givest me much food for thought," said the lawyer.

"Digest it—looking at the reflection of the stars in the water—aye! and recall what is told by Aristotle of Xenophanes, how that casting his eyes upward at the immensity of heaven, he declared *The One* is God. That conviction, at which the philosopher arrived at the summit of his research, is the starting point of the Christian child. Farewell. We shall meet again. I commend thee to Him who set the stars in heaven above, and the lights in thine own dim soul."

Then the bishop sought a boat, and was rowed in the direction of the town.

Æmilius remained by the lagoon.

Words such as these he had heard were novel. The thoughts given him to meditate on were so deep and strange that he could not receive them at once.

The night was now quite dark, and the stars shone with a brilliancy to which we are unaccustomed in the North, save on frosty winter nights.

The Milky Way formed a sort of crescent to the north, and enveloped Cassiopeia's Chair in its nebulous light. To the west blazed Castor and Pollux, and the changing iridescent fire of Algol reflected its varying colors in the water.

Æmilius looked up. What those points of light were, none could say. How was it that they maintained their order of rising and setting? None could answer. Who ruled the planets? That they obeyed a law, was obvious, but by whom was that law imposed?

Æmilius paced quicker, with folded arms and bowed head, looking into the water. The heavens were an unsolved riddle. The earth also was a riddle, without interpretation. Man himself was an enigma, to which there was no solution. Was all in heaven, in earth, to remain thus locked up, unexplained?

How was it that planets and constellations fulfilled the law imposed on them without deviation, and man knew not a law, lived in the midst of a cobweb of guesses, entangling himself in the meshes of vain speculations, and was not shown the commandment he must obey? Why had the Creator implanted in his soul such noble germs, if they were not to fructify—if only to languish for lack of light?

Again he lifted his eyes to the starry vault, and repeated what had been said of Xenophanes, "Gazing on the immensity of heaven, he declared that the One was God." And then, immediately looking down into the depths of his own heart, he added: "And He is reflected here. Would that I knew Him."

Yet how was he to attain the desired knowledge? On all sides were religious quacks offering their nostrums. What guarantee did Christianity offer, that it was other than the wild and empty speculations that swarmed, engaged and disappointed the minds of inquirers?

Unconscious how time passed, Æmilius paced the bank. Then he stood still, looking dreamily over the calm water. A couple of months more and the air would be alive with fire-flies that would cluster on every reed, that would waver in dance above the surface of the lagoon, tens of thousands of drifting stars reflecting themselves in the water, and by their effulgence disturbing the light of the stars also there mirrored.

Thinking of this, Æmilius laughed.

"So is it," said he, "in the world of philosophic thought and religious aspiration. The air is full of fire-flies. They seem to be brilliant torch-bearers assuring us guidance, but they are only vile grubs, and they float above the festering pool that breeds malarial fevers. Where is the truth, where?"

From the distant city sounded a hideous din, like the bellow of a gigantic bull.

Æmilius laughed bitterly.

"I know what that is, it is the voice of the god—so say the priestesses of Nemausus. It is heard at rare intervals. But the mason who made my baths at Ad Fines, explained it to me. He had been engaged on the temple and saw how a brazen instrument like a shell of many convolutions had been contrived in the walls and concealed, so that one woman's breath could sound it and produce such a bellow as would shake the city. Bah! one religion is like another, founded on impostures. What are the stars of heaven but fire-flies of a higher order, of superior flight? We follow them and stumble into the mire, and are engulfed in the slough."

CHAPTER X

LOCUTUS EST!

Every house in Nemausus thrilled with life. Sleep was driven from the drowsiest heads. The tipsy were sobered at once. Those banqueting desisted from conversation. Music was hushed. Men rushed into the street. The beasts in the amphitheater, startled by the strange note, roared and howled. Slowly the chief magistrate rose, sent to summon an edile, and came forth. He was not quick of movement; it took him some time to resolve whether he or his brother magistrate was responsible for order; when he did issue forth, then he found the streets full, and that all men in them were talking excitedly.

The god Nemausus, the *archegos*, the divine founder and ancestor had spoken. His voice was rarely heard. It was told that before the Cimbri and Teutones had swept over the province, he had shouted. That had been in ages past; of late he had been sparing in the exercise of his voice. He was said to have cried out at the great invasion of the

Helvetii, that had been arrested by Julius Cæsar; again to have trumpeted at the outbreak of Civilis and Julius Sabinus, which, however, had never menaced Narbonese Gaul, though at the time the god had called the worst was anticipated. The last time he had been heard was at the revolt of Vindex that preceded the fall of Nero.

Some young skeptics whispered: "By Hercules, the god has a brazen throat."

"It is his hunting horn that peals to call attention. What he will say will be revealed to the priestess."

"Or what the priestess wishes to have believed is his message."

But this incredulous mood was exhibited by very few. None ventured openly to scoff.

"The god hath spoken!" this was the cry through the streets and the forum. Every man asked his fellow what it signified. Some cried out that the prince—the divine Aurelius Antoninus (Caracalla) —had been assassinated, just as he was about to start from Rome for Gaul. Others that the privileges of the city and colony were going to be abrogated. But one said to his fellow, "I augured ill when we heard that the god had been cheated of his due. No marvel he is out of humor, for Perpetua is esteemed the prettiest virgin in Nemausus."

"I wonder that the rescue passed off without notice being taken of the affair by the magistrates."

"Bah! it is the turn of the Petronius Alacinus now, and he will not bestir himself unnecessarily. So long as the public peace be not broken——"

"But it was—there was a riot, a conflict."

"A farcical fight with wind-bags. Not a man was hurt, not a drop of blood flowed. The god will not endure to be balked and his sacrifice made into a jest."

"He is hoarse with rage."

"What does it all mean?"

Then said a stout man: "My good friend, it means that which always happens when the priesthood is alarmed and considers that its power is menaced—its credit is shaken. It will ask for blood."

"There has been a great falling off of late in the worshipers of the gods and in attendance at the games."

"This comes of the spread of the pestilent sect of the Christians. They are the enemies of the human race. They eat little children. The potter Fusius lost his son last week, aged six, and they say it was sacrificed by these sectaries, who stuck needles into it."

"Bah! the body was found in the channel of the stream the child had fallen in."

"I heard it was found half eaten," said a third.

"Rats, rats," explained another standing by.

"Well, these Christians refuse to venerate the images of the Augustus, and therefore are foes to the commonwealth. They should be rooted out."

"You are right there. As to their religious notions—who cares about them? Let them adore what they will—onions like the Egyptians, stars like the Chaldeans, a sword like the Scythians—that is nothing to us; but when they refuse to swear by the Emperor and to offer sacrifice for the welfare of the empire then, I say, they are bad citizens, and should be sent to the lions."

"The lions," laughed the stout man, "seem to respond to the voice, which sounded in their ears, 'Dinner for you, good beasts!' Well, may we have good sport at the games founded by Domitius Afer. I love to lie in bed when the *circius* (mistral) howls and the snowflakes fly. Then one feels snug and enjoys the contrast. So in the amphitheater one realizes the blessedness of life when one looks on at wretches in the hug of the bear, or being mumbled by lions, or played with by panthers."

Perhaps the only man whom the blast did not startle was Tarsius, the inebriated slave, who had been expelled the house of Baudillas, and who was engrossed only with his own wrongs, and who departed swearing that he excommunicated the Church, not the Church him. He muttered threats; he stood haranguing on his own virtues, his piety, his generosity of spirit; he recorded many acts of charity he had done. " And I—I to be turned out! They are a scurvy lot. Not worthy of me. I will start a sect of my own, see if I do not."

Whilst reeling along, growling, boasting, confiding his wrongs to the walls on each side, he ran against Callipodius just as the words were in his mouth: " I am a better Christian than all of them. I don't affect sanctimoniousness in aspect, but I am sound, sound in my life—a plain, straight-walking man."

" Are you so?" asked Callipodius. " Then I wish you would not festoon in such a manner as to lurch against me. You are a Christian. Hard times are coming for such as you."

" Aye, aye! I am a Christian. I don't care who

knows it. I'm not the man to lapse or buy a *libellus*,* though they have turned me out."

Callipodius caught the fellow by the shoulder and shook him.

"Man," said he. "Ah, a slave! I recognize you. You are of the family of Julius Largus Litomarus, the wool merchant. Come with me. The games are in a few days, and the director of the sports has been complaining that he wanted more prisoners to cast to the beasts. I have you in the nick of time. I heard you with these ears confess yourself to be a Christian, and the sole worthy one in the town. You are the man for us—plump and juicy, flushed with wine. By the heavenly twins, what a morsel you will make for the panthers! Come with me. If you resist I will summon the crowd, then perhaps they will elect to have you crucified. Come quietly, and it shall be panthers, not the cross. I will conduct you direct to the magistrate and denounce you."

"I pray you! I beseech you! I was talking

---

* Certain Christians bought substitutes to sacrifice in their room and receive a ticket (*libellus*) certifying that they had sacrificed. The Church was a little perplexed how to deal with these timorous members, who were termed *libellatics*.

nonsense. I was enacting a part for the theater. I am no Christian; I was, but I have been turned out, excommunicated. My master and mistress believe, and just to please them and to escape stripes, and get a few favors such as are not granted to the others, I have—you understand." The slave winked.

Beside Callipodius was a lad bearing a torch. He held it up and the flare fell over the face of the now sobered Tarsius.

"Come with me, fellow," said Callipodius. "Nothing will save you but perfect obedience and compliance with what I direct. Hark! was not that the howl of the beasts. Mehercule! they snuff you already. My good friend Æmilius Lentulus Varo, the lawyer, will be your patron; a strong man. But you must answer my questions. Do you know the Lady Quincta and her daughter? Quincta is the widow of Harpinius Læto."

"Aye, aye! the wench was fished out of the pond to-day."

"That is right. Where are they, do you know their house?"

"Yes, but they are not at home now."

"Where are they then?"

"Will you denounce them?" asked the slave nervously.

"On the contrary. They are menaced. I seek to save them."

"Oh! if that be all, I am your man. They are in the mansion of Baudillas, yonder—that is—but mum, I say! I must not speak. They kicked me out, but I am not ungenerous. I will denounce nobody. But if you want to save the ladies, I will help you with alacrity. They charged me with being drunk—not the ladies—the bishop did that— more shame to him. I but rinsed out my mouth with the Ambrussian. Every drop clear as amber. Ah, sir! in your cellar have you——"

A rush of people up the street shouting, "The will of the god! the will of the god! It is being proclaimed in the forum."

They swept round Callipodius and the slave, spinning them, as leaves are spun in a corner by an eddy of wind, then swept forward in the direction of the great square.

"Come aside with me, fellow," said Callipodius, darting after the slave who was endeavoring to slink away. "What is your name? I know only your face marked by a scar."

"Tarsius, at your service, sir!"

"Good Tarsius, here is money, and I undertake to furnish you with a bottle of my best old Ambrussian for your private tipple, or to make merry therewith with your friends. Be assured, no harm is meant. The priests of Nemausus seek to recover possession of the lady Perpetua, and it is my aim to smuggle her away to a place of security. Do thou watch the door, and I will run and provide litters and porters. Do thou assure the ladies that the litters are sent to convey them in safety to where they will not be looked for; say thy master's house. I will answer for the rest. Hast thou access to them?"

"Aye! I know the pass-word. And though I have been expelled, yet in the confusion and alarm I may be suffered again to enter."

"Very excellent. Thou shalt have thy flask and an ample reward. Say that the litters are sent by thy master, Largus Litomarus."

"Right, sir! I will do thy bidding."

Then Callipodius hastened in the direction of the habitation of Æmilius.

Meanwhile the forum filled with people, crowding on one another, all quivering with excitement.

Above were the stars. Here and there below, torches. Presently the chief magistrate arrived with his lictors, and a maniple of soldiers to keep order and make a passage through the mob between the Temple of Nemausus and the forum.

Few women were present. Such as were, belonged to the lowest of the people. But there were boys and men, old and young, slaves, artisans, freedmen, and citizens.

Among the ignorant and the native population the old Paganism had a strong hold, and their interests attached a certain number of all classes to it. But the popular Paganism was not a religion affecting the lives by the exercise of moral control. It was devoid of any ethic code. It consisted in a system of sacrifice to obtain a good journey, to ward off fevers, to recover bad debts, to banish blight and mildew. The superstitious lived in terror lest by some ill-considered act, by some neglect, they should incur the wrath of the jealous gods and bring catastrophe on themselves or their town. They were easily excited by alarm, and were unreasonable in their selfish fervor.

Ever in anticipation of some disaster, an earthquake, a murrain, fire or pestilence, they were ready, to do whatever they were commanded, so as to avert danger from themselves. The words of the Apostle to the Hebrews describing the Gentiles as being through fear of death all their lifetime subject to bondage, were very true. The ignorant and superstitious may be said to have existed on the verge of a panic, always in terror lest their gods should hurt them, and cringing to them in abject deprecation of evil. It was this fear for themselves and their substance that rendered them cruel.

The procession came from the temple. Torches were borne aloft, a long wavering line of lurid fire, and vessels were carried in which danced lambent flames that threw out odoriferous fumes.

First came the priests; they walked with their heads bowed and their arms folded across their breasts, and with fillets of wool around their heads. Then followed the priestesses shrouded in sable mantles over their white tunics. All moved in silence. A hush fell on the multitude. Nothing was heard in the stillness save the tramp of feet in rhythm. When the procession had reached the forum, the chief priestess ascended the rostrum, and the flambeau-bearers ranged themselves in a half-circle below. She was a tall, splendidly formed woman, with profuse dark hair, an ivory complexion, flashing black eyes under heavy brows.

Suddenly she raised her arms and extended them, letting the black pall drop from her shoulders, and reveal her in a woven silver robe, like a web of moonlight, and with white bare arms. In her right she bore an ivory silver-bound wand with mistletoe bound about it, every berry of translucent stone.

Then amidst dead silence she cried: "The god hath spoken, he who founded this city, from whom are sprung its ancient patrician families, who supplieth you with crystal water from his urn. The holy one demands that she who hath been taken from him be surrendered to him again, and that punishment be inflicted on the Christians who have desecrated his statue. If this, his command, be not fulfilled, then will he withhold the waters, and deliver over the elect city to be a desolation, the haunt of the lizard and the owl and bat. To the lions with the Christians! *Locutus est Divus Archegos!*"

CHAPTER XI

PALANQUINS

With the exception of the bishop, Marcianus, and a few others, all assembled at the Agape were struck with the liveliest terror. They entertained no doubt but that the sound that shook the walls was provoked by the outrage on the image of the tutelary god, following on the rescue of the victim alloted to him.

The pagan inhabitants of Nemausus were roused to exasperation. The priesthood would employ every available means to work this resentment to a paroxysm, and the result would be riot and murder, perhaps an organized persecution.

It must be understood that although the Roman State recognized other religions than the established paganism, as that of the Jews, and allowed the votaries freedom of worship, yet Christianity was not of this number. It was in itself illegal, and any magistrate, at his option, in any place and at any time, might put the laws in force against the members of the Church. Not only so, but any envious, bigoted, or resentful person might compel a magistrate to take cognizance of the presence of Christians in the district under his jurisdiction, and require him to capitally convict those brought before him.

The system in the Roman Commonwealth for the maintenance of order was that every man was empowered to act as spy upon and delate another. Any man might accuse his neighbor, his brother, before the court; and if he could prove his charge, the magistrate had no option—he must sentence. Consequently the Christians depended for their safety on the favor of their fellow-citizens, on their own abstention from giving offence.

The sole protection against false accusations in the Roman Commonwealth lay in the penalties to which an accuser was subject should he fail to establish his charge. But as on conviction a portion of the estate of the guilty person was handed over to the accuser, there was an inducement to delation.

Under the Julian and Claudian Cæsars the system had worked terribly. An entire class of men made denunciation their trade. They grew rich on the spoils of their victims, they spared none, and the judges themselves lived in fear of them. The evil became so intolerable that measures were taken to accentuate the risk to the accusers. If the Christians were not oftener denounced, the reason was that in the event of one lapsing, and through terror or pain abjuring Christ, then immediately the tables were turned, and the accuser was placed in danger of his life.

When an Emperor issued an edict against the Christians he enacted no new law; he merely required that the exisiting laws should be put in force against them, and all risk to delators was removed in that no delation was exacted. On such an occasion every citizen and householder was required to appear before the court and offer a few grains of incense on an altar to the genius of the empire or of the prince. Should any one refuse to do this, then he was convicted of high treason and delivered over to the executioner to be either tortured or put to death off-hand. When the magistrate deemed it important to obtain a recantation, then he had recourse to the rack, iron hooks, torches, thumbscrews as means of forcing the prisoner through pain to abjure Christ.

The Christians in Nemausus had lived in complete tranquillity. There had been no persecution. They had multiplied.

The peace enjoyed by the Church had been to it of a mixed advantage. Many had been included whose conversion was due to questionable motives. Some had joined through sincere conviction; more from conviction seasoned with expectation of advantage. The poor had soon learned that a very rich and abundant stream of charity flowed in the Church, that in it the sick and feeble were cared for and their necessities were supplied, whereas in the established paganism no regard was paid to the needy and suffering. Among the higher classes there were adherents who attached themselves to the Church rather because they disbelieved in heathenism than that they held to the Gospel. Some accepted the truth with the head, but their hearts remained untouched.

None had given freer expression to his conviction that there were weak-kneed and unworthy members than Marcianus the deacon. He had remonstrated with the bishop, he had scolded, repelled, but without effect. And now he had taken a daring step, the consequence of which would be that the members of the community would indeed be put to the test whether they were for Christ or Mammon. The conviction that a time of trial was come broke on the community like a thundercloud, and produced a panic. Many doubted their constancy, all shrank from being brought to a trial of their faith. The congregation in the house of Baudillas, when it had recovered from the first shock, resolved itself into groups agitated by various passions. Some launched into recrimination against Marcianus, who had brought them into jeopardy; some consulted in whispers how to escape the danger; a few fell into complete stupefaction of mind, unable to decide on any course. Others, again, abandoned themselves to despair and shrieked forth hysterical lamentations. Some crowded around Castor, clung to his garments and entreated him to save them. Others endeavored to escape from a place and association that would compromise them, by the back entrance to the servants' portion of the house.

A few, a very few maintained their composure, and extending their arms fell to prayer.

Baudillas hurried from one party to another uttering words of reassurance, but his face was blanched, his voice quivered, and he was obviously employing formal expressions that conveyed no strength to his own heart. Marcianus, with folded arms, looked at him scornfully, and as he passed, said, "The bishop should not have ordained such an unstable and quaking being as thyself to serve in the sacred ministry."

"Ah, brother," sighed Baudillas, "it is with me as with Peter. The spirit truly is willing, but the flesh is weak."

"That was spoken of him," answered Marcianus, "before Pentecost and the outpouring of the spirit of strength. Such timidity, such feebleness are unworthy of a Christian."

"Pray for me that my faith fail not," said Baudillas, and passed on. By action he deadened his fears. Now came in Pedo, the old servant of the house, who had been sent forth to reconnoiter. His report was not reassuring. The mob was sweeping through the streets, and insisting on every household producing an image at its doors and placing a light before it. There were fuglemen who directed the crowd, which had been divided into bands to perambulate every division of the town and make inquisition of every house. The mob had begun by breaking into such dwellings as were not protected by an image, and wrecking them. But after one or two of such acts of violence, the magistrates had interfered, and although they suffered the people to assemble before the houses and to clamor for the production of an image and a light, yet they sent *vigiles* (*i.e.*, the watch) to guard such dwellings as remained undecorated. When the master of the house refused obedience to the mandate of the mob, then an officer ordered him to open the door, and he summoned him to appear next day in court and there do sacrifice. By this means the mob was satisfied and passed on without violence.

But as the crowd marched down the streets it arrested every man and woman that was encountered, and insisted on their swearing by the gods and blaspheming Christ.

Castor ordered the congregation to depart by twos and by threes, to take side alleys, and to avoid the main thoroughfares. This was possible, as the *posticum*, a back door, communicated with a mean street that had the city wall for one side.

"My sons and daughters in Christ," said the bishop with composure, "remember that greater is He that is with us than those that be against us. When the servant of Elisha feared, then the Lord opened his eyes that he might behold the angels with chariots and horses of fire prepared to defend His servant. Avoid danger, but if it cannot be avoided stand firm. Remember His words, 'He that confesseth me before men, him will I also confess before my Father which is in heaven.'"

As soon as all had departed, but not till then, did Castor leave. Marcianus turned with a sneer to his fellow-deacon and said, "Fly! you have full license from the bishop; and he sets the example himself."

"I must tarry in my own house," answered Baudillas. "I have the ladies Quincta and Perpetua under my protection. They cannot return to their home until they be fetched."

"So! they lean on a broken reed such as thee!"

"Alack! they have none other to trust to."

"The mob is descending our street," cried the slave, Pedo, limping in.

"What are we to do?" asked Quincta trembling. "If they discover me and my daughter here we are undone. They will tear her from my arms."

The deacon Baudillas, clasped his hands to his head. Then his slave said: "Master, Tarsius is at the door with litters and bearers. He saith he hath been sent for the lady Perpetua."

"And for me?" asked Quincta eagerly.

"And for thee also, lady. It is said that guards are observing thy house and that, therefore, thy slaves cannot venture hither. Therefore, so says

Tarsius, his master, the wool-merchant, Julius Largus, hath sent his litters and porters."

"But his house will be visited!"

"The bearers have instructions as to what shall be done."

"This is strange," said Quincta. "I did not suppose that Largus Litomarus would have shown such consideration. We are not acquainted—indeed we belong to different classes——"

"Yet are ye one in Christ," said the deacon. "Call in Tarsius, he shall explain the matter. But let him be speedy or the rabble will be on us."

"They are at the head of the street," said the slave, "and visit the door of Terentius Cominius."

"He believes."

"And he has set out a figure of the Good Shepherd before his door with a lamp. The crowd regards it as a Mercury and has cheered and gone on to the next door."

Tarsius, thoroughly recovered from his intoxication, was now admitted. He looked none in the face, and stumbled through his tale. Julius Largus Litomarus had bidden him offer his litters; there were curtains closing them, and his servants would convey the ladies to a place of security.

Quincta was too frightened, too impatient to be off, to question the man, nor was the deacon more nice in inquiry, for he also was in a condition of nervous unrest.

The shouts of the mob could be heard.

"I do not wholly trust this man," said Baudillas. "He was expelled for misconduct. Yet, what can we do? Time presses! Hark!—in a brief space the rabble will be here. Next house is a common lodging and will not detain them. Would that Marcianus had remained. He could have advised us. Madam, act as you think best."

"The mob is on the move," said Pedo. "They have been satisfied at the house of Dulcius Liber, and now Septimus Philadelphus is bringing out half-a-dozen gods. Master—there is not a moment to be lost."

"Let us fly—quick!" gasped Quincta.

She plucked her daughter's arm, and fairly dragged her along the passage out of the house.

In the street they saw a flare. The rabble, held in control by some directing spirit, was furnished with torches. It was roaring outside a house, impatient because no statue was produced, and proceeded to throw stones and batter the door.

"That house is empty," whispered Pedo. "The master was bankrupt and everything sold. There is not a person in it."

Quincta mounted the *lectica* or palanquin that was offered, without looking whether her daughter were safe, and allowed the bearers, nay urged them, to start at a trot.

Tarsius remained behind. He handed Perpetua into the second closed litter, then gave the word, and ran beside it, holding the curtains together with one hand.

Baudillas trembling for himself was now left alone.

CHAPTER XII

REUS

"Master!" said the old slave, moving uneasily on his stiff joint, before the even more nervously agitated master, "Master, there is the freedwoman Glyceria below, who comes in charing. She has brought an idol of Tarranus under her cloak, and offers to set that with a lamp before the door. She is not a believer, she worships devils, but is a good soul and would save us. She awaits your permission."

The deacon was profoundly moved.

"It must not be! It may not be! I—I am a deacon of the Church. This is known to be a Christian household. The Church is in my house, and here the divine mysteries are celebrated. If she had not asked my leave, and had—if—but no, I cannot sanction this. God strengthen me, I am distracted and weak." The slave remained. He expected that his master in the end would yield.

"And yet," stammered Baudillas, "He hath compassion on the infirm and feeble. He forgave Peter. May He not pardon me if—? Glyceria is a heathen woman. She does not belong to my family. I did not propose this. I am not responsible for her acts. But no—it would be a betrayal of the truth, a dishonor to the Church. He that confesseth me before men—no, no, Pedo, it may not be."

"And now it is too late," said the slave. "They are at the door."

Blows resounded through the house, and the roar of voices from the street surged up over the roof, and poured in through the opening over the *impluvium*. It was as though a mighty sea were thundering against the house and the waves curled over it and plunged in through the gap above the court.

"You must open, Pedo. I will run upstairs for a moment and compose myself. Then—if it must be—but do not suffer the rabble to enter. If a prefect be there, or his underling and soldiers, let them keep the door. Say I shall be down directly. Yet stay—is the *posticum* available for escape?"

"Sir—the mob have detailed a party to go to the backs of the houses and watch every way of exit."

"Then it is God's will that I be taken. I cannot help myself. I am glad I said No to the offer of Glyceria."

The deacon ascended a flight of limestone steps to the upper story. The slabs were worn and cracked, and had not been repaired owing to his poverty. He entered a room that looked out on the street, and went to the window.

The street above his doorway was dense with people, below it was completely empty. Torches threw up a glare illumining the white façades of the houses. He saw a sea of heads below. He heard the growl of voices breaking into a foam of coarse laughter. Curses uttered against the Christians, blasphemies against Christ, words of foulness, threats, brutal jests, formed the matter of the hubbub below. A man bearing a white wand with a sprig of artificial mistletoe at the end, gave directions to the people where to go, where to stop, what to do. He was the head of the branch of the guild of the Cultores Nemausi for that portion of the town.

Someone in the mob lifting his face, looked up and saw the deacon at the window, and at once shouted, "There! there he is! Baudillas Macer, come down, sacrilegious one! That is he who carried the maiden away."

Then rose hoots and yells, and a boy putting his hands together and blowing produced an unearthly scream.

"He is one of them! He is a ringleader! He has an ass's head in the house to which he sacrifices our little ones. He it was who stuck needles into the child of the potter Fusius, and then gnawed off the cheeks and fingers. He can inform where is the daughter of Aulus Harpinius who was snatched from the basin of the god. Let us avenge on him the great sacrilege that has been committed. It was he who struck off the head of the god."

Then one flung a stone that crashed into the room, and had not Baudillas drawn back, it would have struck and thrown him down stunned.

"Let the house be ransacked!" yelled the mob. "We will seek in it for the bones of the murdered children. Break open the door if he will not unfasten. Bring a ladder, we will enter by the windows. Someone ascend to the roof and drop into the *atrium*."

Then ensued a rush against the valves, but they were too solid to yield; and the bars held them firm, run as they were into their sockets in the solid wall.

The slave Pedo now knocked on the inside. This was the signal that he was about to open.

The soldiers drew up across the entrance, and when the door was opened, suffered none to enter the house save the deputy of the prefect with four of his police, and some of the leaders of the Cultores Nemausi. And now a strange calm fell on the hitherto troubled spirit of Baudillas. He was aware that no effort he could make would enable him to escape. His knees, indeed, shook under him as he went to the stairs to descend, and forgetting that the tenth step was broken, he stumbled at it and was nearly precipitated to the bottom. Yet all wavering, all hesitation in his mind was at an end.

He saw the men in the court running about, calling to each other, peering into every room, cubicle, and closet; one called that the cellar was the place in which the infamous rites of the Christians were performed and that there would be found amphoræ filled with human blood. Then one shouted that in the *tablinum* there was naught save a small table. Immediately after a howl rose from those who had penetrated to the *triclinium*, and next moment they came rushing forth in such excitement that they dragged down the curtain that hung before the door and entangled their feet in it. One, not staying to disengage himself, held up his hands and exhibited the broken head of the statue, that had been brought there by Marcianus, and by him left on the floor.

"It is he who has done it! The sacrilegious one! The defacer of the holy image!" howled the men, and fell upon the deacon with their fists. Some plucked at his hair; one spat in his face. Others kicked him, and tripping him up, cast him his length on the ground, where they would have beaten and trampled the life out of him, had not the deputy of the ædile interfered, rescued him from the hands of his assailants and thrust him into a chamber at the side of the hall, saying: "He shall be brought before the magistrate. It is not for you to take into your hands the execution of criminals untried and uncondemned."

Then one of the officers of the club ran to the doorway of the house, and cried: "Citizens of Nemausus, hearken. The author of the egregious impiety has been discovered. It is Cneius Baudillas Macer, who belongs to an ancient, though decayed, family of this town. He who should have been the last to dishonor the divine founder has raised his parricidal hand against him. He stands convicted. The head of the god has been found in the house; it is that recently broken off from the statue by the baths. Eheu! Eheu! Woe be to the city, unless this indignity be purged away."

A yell of indignation rose as an answer.

The slave Pedo was suffered to enter the bedroom, on the floor of which lay his master bruised and with his face bleeding; for some of his front teeth had been broken and his lips were cut.

" Oh master! dear master! What is to be done?" asked the faithful creature, sobbing in his distress.

"I wonder greatly, Pedo, how I have endured so much. My fear is lest in the end I fall away. I enjoin you—there is naught else you can do for me—seek the bishop, and ask that the prayers of the Church may go up to the Throne of Grace for me. I am feeble and frail. I was a frightened shy lad in old times. If I were to fall, it would be a shame to the Church of God in this town, this Church that has so many more worthy than myself in it."

" Can I bring thee aught, master? Water and a towel?"

"Nay, nothing, Pedo! Do as I bid. It is all that I now desire."

The soldiers entered, raised the deacon, and made him walk between them. A man was placed in front, another behind to protect him against the people. As Baudillas was conveyed down the *ostium*, the passage to the door, he could see faces glowering in at him; he heard angry voices howling at him; an involuntary shrinking came over him, but he was irresistibly drawn forward by the soldiers. On being thrust through the doorway before all, then a great roar broke forth, fists and sticks were shaken at him, but none ventured to cast stones lest the soldiers should be struck.

One portion of the mob now detached itself from the main body, so as to follow and surround the deacon and assure itself that he did not escape before he was consigned to the prison.

The city of Nemausus, capital of the Volcæ Arecomici, though included geographically in the province of Narbonese Gaul, was in fact an independent republic, not subject to the proconsul, but under Roman suzerainty. With twenty-four *comæ* or townships under it, it governed itself by popular election, and enjoyed the *lex Italica*. This little republic was free from land tax, and it was governed by four functionaries, the Quatuor-viri, two of whom looked after the finances, and two, like the *duumviri* elsewhere, were for the purpose of maintaining order, and the criminal jurisdiction was in their hands. Their title in full was *duum viri juri dicendo*, and they were annually elected by the senate. Their function was much that in small of the Roman consuls, and they were sometimes in joke entitled consuls. They presided over the senate and had the government of the town and state in their hands during their tenure of office. On leaving their office they petitioned for and received the right to ride horses, and were accounted knights. They wore the dignified *præ texta*, and were attended by two lictors.

Baudillas walked between his escort. He was in a dazed condition. The noise, the execrations cast at him, the flashing of the torches on the helmets and breastplates of the guard, the glittering eyes and teeth of the faces peering at him, the pain from the contusions he had received combined to bewilder him. In the darkness and confusion of his brain, but one thought remained permanent and burnt like a brilliant light, his belief in Christ, and one desire occupied his soul, to be true to his faith. He was too distracted to pray. He could not rally his senses nor fix his ideas, but the yearning of his humble soul rose up, like the steam from a new turned glebe in the sun of a spring morning.

In times of persecution certain strong spirits had rushed to confession and martyrdom in an intoxication of zeal, such as Baudillas could not understand. He did not think of winning the crown of martyrdom, but he trembled lest he should prove a castaway.

Thrust forward, dragged along, now stumbling, then righted by the soldiers sustaining him, Baudillas was conveyed to the forum and to the basilica where the magistrate was seated.

On account of the disturbance, the Duum-vir— we will so term him though he was actually one of the Quatuor-viri—he whose turn it was to maintain order and administer justice, had taken his place in the court, so as to be able to consign to custody such as were brought in by the guard on suspicion of being implicated in the outrage; he was there as well for the purpose of being ready to take measures promptly should the mob become unmanageable. So long as it was under control, he did not object to its action, but he had no thought of letting it get the upper hand. Rioters, like children, have a liking for fire, and if they were suffered to apply their torches to the houses of Christians might produce a general conflagration.

Although the magistrates were chosen by popular election, it was not those who constituted the rabble who had votes, and had to be humored, but the citizen householders, who viewed the upheaval of the masses with jealous suspicion.

That the proceedings should be conducted in an orderly manner, instructions had been issued that no arrest was to be made without there being someone forthcoming to act as accuser, and the soldiers were enjoined to protect whosoever was menaced against whom no one was prepared to formulate a charge which he would sustain in court.

In the case of Baudillas there would be no difficulty. The man—he was the treasurer of the guild—who had found the mutilated head was ready to appear against him.

The court into which the deacon was brought rapidly filled with a crowd, directly he had been placed in what we should now call the dock. Then the accuser stood up and gave his name. The magistrate accepted the accusation. Whereupon the accuser made oath that he acted from no private motive of hostility to the accused, and that he was not bribed by a third person to delate him. This done, he proceeded to narrate how he had entered the house of Baudillas, surnamed Macer, who was generally believed to be a minister of the sect of the Christians; how that in searching the house he had lighted on a mutilated head on the pavement of the *triclinium*. He further stated that he well knew the statue of the god Nemausus that stood by the fountain which supplied the lower town, and that he was firmly convinced that the head which he now produced had belonged to the statue, which statue had that very night been wantonly and impiously defaced. He therefore concluded that the owner of the house, Baudillas Macer, was either directly or indirectly guilty of the act of sacrilege, and he demanded his punishment in accordance with the law.

This sufficed as preliminary.

Baudillas was now *reus*, and as such was ordered to be conveyed to prison, there to be confined until the morning, when the interrogation would take place.

CHAPTER XIII

AD FINES

Perpetua was carried along at a swinging trot in the closed litter, till the end of the street had been reached, and then, after a corner had been turned, the bearers relaxed their pace. It was too dark for her to see what were the buildings past which she was taken, even had she withdrawn the curtains that shut in the litter; but to withdraw these curtains would have required her to exert some force, as they were held together in the grasp of Tarsius, running and striding at the side. But, indeed, she did not suppose it necessary to observe the direction in which she was being conveyed. She had accepted in good faith the assurance that the *lectica* had been sent by the rich Christian wool merchant, Largus Litomarus, and had acquiesced in her mother's readiness to accept the offer, without a shadow of suspicion.

God had delivered her from a watery death, and she regarded the gift as one to be respected; her life thus granted her was not to be wilfully thrown away or unnecessarily jeopardized. Unless she escaped from the house of the deacon, she would fall into the hands of the rabble, and this was a prospect more terrifying than any other. If called upon again to witness a good confession, she would do so, God helping her, but she was glad to be spared the ordeal.

It was not till the porters halted, and knocked at a door, and she had descended from the palanquin, that some suspicion crossed her mind that all was not right. She looked about her, and inquired for her mother. Then one whom she had not hitherto noticed drew nigh, bowing, and said: "Lady, your youthful and still beautiful mother will be here presently. The slaves who carry her have gone about another way so as to divert attention from your priceless self, should any of the mob have set off in pursuit."

The tone of the address surprised the girl. Her mother was not young, and although in her eyes that mother was lovely, yet Quincta was not usually approached with expressions of admiration for her beauty.

Again Perpetua accepted what was said, as the reason given was plausible, and entered the house.

The first thing she observed, by the torch glare, was a statue of Apollo. She was surprised, and inquired, hesitatingly, "Is this the house of Julius Largus Litomarus?"

"Admirable is your ladyship's perspicuity. Even in the dark those more-than-Argus eyes discern the truth. The worthy citizen Largus belongs to the sect. He is menaced as well as other excellent citizens by the unreasoning and irrational vulgar. He has therefore instructed that you should be conveyed to the dwelling of a friend, only deploring that it should be unworthy of your presence."

"May I ask your name, sir?"

"Septimus Callipodius, at your service."

"I do not remember to have heard the name, but," she added with courtesy, "that is due to my ignorance as a young girl, or to my defective memory."

"It is a name that has not deserved to be harbored in the treasury of such a mind."

The girl was uneasy. The fulsome compliment and the obsequious bow of the speaker were not merely repugnant to her good taste, but filled her with vague misgivings. It was true that exaggeration and flattery in address were common enough at the period, but not among Christians, who abstained from such extravagance. The mode of speaking adopted by Callipodius stamped him as not being one of the faithful.

"I will summon a female slave to attend on your ladyship," said he; "and she will conduct you to the women's apartments. Ask for whatever you desire. The entire contents of the house are at your disposal."

"I prefer to remain here in the court till my mother shall arrive."

"Alas! adorable lady! it is possible that you may have to endure her absence for some time. Owing to the disturbed condition of the streets, it is to be feared that her carriage has been stopped; it is not unlikely that she may have been compelled to take refuge elsewhere; but, under no circumstances short of being absolutely prevented from joining you, will she fail to meet you to-morrow in the villa Ad Fines."

"Whose villa?"

"The villa to which, for security, you and your mother the Lady Quincta are to be conveyed till the disturbances are over, and the excitement in men's minds has abated. By Hercules! one might say that the drama of the quest of Proserpine by Ceres were being rehearsed, were it not that the daughter is seeking the mother as well as the latter her incomparable child."

"I cannot go to Ad Fines without her."

"Lady, in all humility, as unworthy to advise you in anything, I would venture to suggest that your safety depends on accepting the means of escape that are offered. The high priestess has declared that nothing will satisfy the incensed god but that you should be surrendered to her, and what mercy you would be likely to encounter at her hands, after what has taken place, your penetrating mind will readily perceive. Such being the case, I dare recommend that you snatch at the opportunity offered, fly the city and hide in the villa of a friend who will die rather than surrender you. None will suspect that you are there."

"What friend? Largus Litomarus is scarcely to be termed an acquaintance of my mother."

"Danger draws close all generous ties," said Callipodius.

"But my mother?"

"Your mother, gifted with vast prudence, may have judged that her presence along with you would increase the danger to yourself. I do not say so. But it may so happen that her absence at this moment may be due to her good judgment. On the other hand, it may also have chanced, as I already intimated, that her litter has been stayed, and she has been constrained to sacrifice."

"That she will never do."

"In that case, I shudder at the consequences. But why suppose the worst? She has been delayed. And now, lady, suffer me to withdraw—it is an eclipse of my light to be beyond the radiance of your eyes. I depart, however, animated by the conviction, and winging my steps, that I go to perform your dearest wish—to obtain information relative to your lady mother, and to learn when and where she will rejoin you. Be ready to start at dawn—as soon as the city gates are opened, and that will be in another hour."

Then Perpetua resigned herself to the female servants, who led her into the inner and more private portions of the house, reached by means of a passage called " the Jaws " (*fauces*).

Perpetua was aware that she was in a difficult situation, one in which she was unable to know how she was placed, and from which she could not extricate herself. She was young and inexperienced, and, on the whole, inclined to trust what she was told.

In pagan Rome, it was not customary for girls to be allowed the liberty that alone could give them self-confidence. Perhaps the condition of that evil world was such that this would not have been possible. When the foulest vice flaunted in public without a blush, when even religion demoralized, then a Roman parent held that the only security for the innocence of a daughter lay in keeping her closely guarded from every corrupting sight and sound. She was separated from her brothers and from all men; she associated with her mother and with female slaves only. She was hardly allowed in the street or road, except in a litter with curtains close drawn, unless it were at some religious festival or public ceremony, when she was attended by her relatives and not allowed out of their sight.

This was due not merely to the fact that evil was rampant, but also to the conviction in the hearts of parents that innocence could be preserved only by ignorance. They were unable to supply a child with any moral principle, to give it any law for the government of life, which would plant the best guardian of virtue within, in the heart.

Augustus, knowing of no divine law, elevated sentimental admiration for the simplicity of the ancients into a principle—only to discover that it was inadequate to bear the strain put on it; that the young failed to comprehend why they should control their passions and deny themselves pleasures out of antiquarian pedantry. Marcus Aurelius had sought in philosophy a law that would keep life pure and noble, but his son Commodus cast philosophy to the winds as a bubble blown by the breath of man, and became a monster of vice. Public opinion was an unstable guide. It did worse than fluctuate, it sank. Much was tolerated under the Empire that was abhorrent to the conscience under the Republic. It allowed to-day what it had condemned yesterday. It was a nose of wax molded by the vicious governing classes, accommodated to their license.

Although a Christian maiden was supplied with that which the most exalted philosophy could not furnish—a revealed moral code, descending from the Creator of man for the governance of man, yet Christian parents could not expose their children to contamination of mind by allowing them the wide freedom given at this day to an English or American girl. Moreover, the customs of social life had to be complied with, and could not be broken through. Christian girls were accordingly still under some restraint, were kept dependent on their parents, and were not allowed those opportunities for free action which alone develop individuality and give independence of character. Nevertheless, in times of persecution, when many of these maidens thus closely watched were brought to the proof of their faith, they proved as strong as men—so mighty was the grace of God, so stubborn was faith.

Although Perpetua was greatly exhausted by the strain to which she had been exposed during the day, she could not rest when left to herself in a quiet room, so alarmed was she at the absence of her mother.

An hour passed, then a second. Finally, steps sounded in the corridor before her chamber, and she knew that she must rise from the couch on which she had cast herself and continue her flight.

A slave presented herself to inform Perpetua that Callipodius had returned with the tidings that her mother was unable at once to rejoin her, that she was well and safe, and had preceded her to Ad Fines; that she desired her daughter to follow with the utmost expedition, and that she was impatient to embrace her. The slave woman added that the streets were now quiet, the city gates were open, and that the litter was at the door in readiness.

"I will follow you with all speed. Leave me to myself."

Then, when the slave had withdrawn, Perpetua hastily arranged her ruffled hair, extended her arms, and turning to the east, invoked the protection of the God who had promised, "I will never leave thee, nor forsake thee."

On descending to the *atrium*, Perpetua knelt by the water-tank and bathed her face and neck. Then she mounted the litter that awaited her outside the house. The bearers at once started at a run, nor did they desist till they had passed through the city gate on the road that led to the mountain range of the Cebennæ. This was no military way, but it led into the pleasant country where the citizens of Nemausus and some of the rich merchants of Narbo had their summer quarters.

The gray dawn had appeared. Market people from the country were coming into the town with their produce in baskets and carts.

The bearers jogged along till the road ascended

with sufficient rapidity to make them short of breath. The morning was cold. A streak of light lay in the east, and the wind blew fresh from the same quarter. The colorless white dawn overflowed the plain of the Rhodanus, thickly strewn with olives, whose gray foliage was much of the same tint as the sky overhead. To the south and southeast the olive plantations were broken by tracts of water, some permanent lagoons, others due to recent inundations. To the right, straight as an arrow, white as snow, ran the high road from Italy to Spain, that crossed the Rhodanus at Ugernum, the modern Beaucaire, and came from Italy by Tegulata, the scene of the victory of Marius over the Cimbri, and by Aquæ Sextiæ and its hot springs.

The journey was long; the light grew. Presently the sun rose and flushed all with light and heat. The chill that had penetrated to the marrow of the drowsy girl gave way. She had refused food before starting; now, when the bearers halted at a little wayside tavern for refreshment and rest, she accepted some cakes and spiced wine from the fresh open-faced hostess with kindly eyes and a pleasant smile, and felt her spirits revive. Was she not to rejoin her dear mother? Had she not escaped with her life from extreme peril? Was she not going to a place where she would be free from pursuit?

She continued her journey with a less anxious heart. The scenery improved, the heights were wooded, there were juniper bushes, here and there tufts of pale helebore.

Then the litter was borne on to a terrace before a mass of limestone crag and forest that rose in the rear. A slave came to the side of the palanquin and drew back the curtain. Perpetua saw a bright pretty villa, with pillars before it forming a peristyle. On the terrace was a fountain plashing in a basin.

"Lady," said the slave, "this is Ad Fines. The master salutes you humbly, and requests that you will enter."

"The master? What master?"

"Æmilius Lentulus Varo."

CHAPTER XIV

TO THE LOWEST DEPTH

Baudillas found that there were already many in the prison, who had been swept together by the mob and the soldiers, either for having refused to produce an image, or for having declined to sacrifice. To his no small surprise he saw among them the wool-merchant Julius Largus Litomarus. The crowd had surrounded his house, and as he had not complied with their demands, they had sent him to the duumvir,* Petronius Atacinus, who had consigned him to prison till, at his leisure, he could investigate the charge against him.

The two magistrates who sat in court and gave sentence were Petronius Atacinus and Vibius Fuscianus, and they took it in turns to sit, each being the acting magistrate for a month, when he was succeeded by the other. Atacinus was a humane man, easy-going, related to the best families in the place,

---

* I employ the term Duumvir for convenience. As already stated, there were four chief magistrates, but two only had criminal jurisdiction.

and acquainted with such as he was not allied with by blood or marriage. His position, in face of the commotion relative to the mutilation of the image and the rescue of Perpetua, was not an easy one.

In Rome and in every other important city, the *flamen*, or chief priest, occupied a post of considerable importance and influence. He sat in the seat at the games and in the theater next to the chief magistrates, and took precedence over every other officer in the town. Nemausus had such a *flamen*, and he was not only the official religious head in the place, but was also the *flamen Augustalis*, the pontiff connected with the worship of Augustus, which had become the predominant cult in Narbonese Gaul, and also head of the College of the Augustals, that comprised the very powerful body of freedmen. The priestess of the divine founder and giver of the fountain shared his dignity and authority. Between them they could exercise a preponderating power in the town, and it would be in vain for Petronius Atacinus, however easy-going he might be, and disinclined to shed blood, to pass over what had been done without affording satisfaction to the pagan party moved and held together by the priesthood.

Yet the duumvir judged that it would be eminently unadvisable for him to proceed with too great severity, and to punish too many persons. Christianity had many adherents in the place, and some of these belonged to the noble, others to the mercantile, families. The general wish among the well-to-do was that there should be no systematic persecution. An inquisitorial search after Christians would break up families, rouse angry passions, and, above all, disturb business.

Petronius had already resolved on his course. He had used every sort of evasion that could be practiced. He had knowingly abstained from enjoining on the keepers of the city gates the requisition of a passport from such as left the town. The more who fled and concealed themselves, the better pleased would he be.

Nevertheless, he had no thought of allowing the mutilation of the statue to pass unpunished, and he was resolved on satisfying the priesthood by restoring Perpetua to them. If he were obliged to put any to death, he would shed the blood only of such as were inconsiderable and friendless.

There was another element that entered into the matter, and which helped to render Atacinus inclined to leniency. The Cæsar at the time was M.

Aurelius Antoninus, commonly known as Caracalla. He had been brought up from infancy by a Christian nurse, and was thought to harbor a lurking regard for the members of the religion of Christ. At any rate, he displayed no intolerance towards those who professed it. He was, himself, a ferocious tyrant, as capricious as he was cruel. He had murdered his brother Geta in a fit of jealousy, and his conscience, tortured by remorse, drove him to seek relief by prying into the mysteries of strange religions.

The duumvir Atacinus was alive to the inclinations and the temper of the prince, and was the more afraid of offending him by persecution of the Christians, as the Emperor was about shortly to visit Gaul, and might even pass through Nemausus.

If in such a condition of affairs the Christians were exposed to danger, it may well be inferred that, where it was less favorable, their situation was surrounded with danger. They were at all times liable to fall victims to popular tumults, occasioned sometimes by panic produced by an earthquake, by resentment at an accidental conflagration which the vulgar insisted on referring to the Christians, sometimes by distress at the breaking out of an epidemic.

On such occasions the unreasoning rabble clamored that the gods were incensed at the spread of the new atheism, and that the Christians must be cast to the lions.

When Baudillas saw the wool merchant in the prison, he went to him immediately. Litomarus was sitting disconsolately on a stone bench with his back against the prison wall.

"I did not go to the Agape," said he; "I was afraid to do so. But I might as well. The people bellowed under my windows like bulls of Bashan."

"And you did not exhibit an image?"

"No, I could not do that. Then the *viatores* of the ædiles took me in charge. I was hustled about, and was dragged off here. My wife fell down in a faint. I do not think she will recover the shock. She has been in a weak condition ever since the death of our little Cordula. We loved that child. We were wrapped up in her. Marcianus said that we made of the little creature an earthly idol, and that it was right she should be taken away. I do not know. She had such winning ways. One could not help loving her. She made such droll remarks, and screwed up her little eyes——"

"But before you were arrested, you thought considerately of Perpetua and her mother Quincta."

"I do not understand to what you refer."

"To the sending of litters for them."

"I sent no litters."

"Your slave Tarsius came to my house to announce that you had been pleased to remember the ladies there taking refuge, and that you had placed your two palanquins at their disposal."

"Tarsius said this?"

"Even Tarsius."

"Tarsius is a slippery rascal. He was very fond of our little Cordula, and was wont to carry her on his shoulder, so we have liked him because of that. Nevertheless, he is—well, not trustworthy."

"May God avert that a trap has been laid to ensnare the virgin and her mother. Tarsius was expelled the Church for inebriety."

"I know nothing about the palanquins. I have but one. After the death of little Cordula, I did not care to keep a second. I always carry about with me a lock cut from her head after death. It is like floss silk."

The wool merchant was too greatly absorbed in his own troubles to give attention to the matter that had been broached by the deacon. Baudillas withdrew to another part of the prison in serious concern.

When day broke, Litomarus was released. His brother was a pagan and had easily satisfied the magistrate. This brother was in the firm, and traveled for it, buying fleeces from the shepherds on the limestone plateaux of Niger and Larsacus. He had been away the day before, but on his return in the morning, on learning that Julius was arrested, he spoke with the duumvir, presented him with a ripe ewe's milk cheese just brought by him from Larsacus, and obtained the discharge of Julius without further difficulty.

Baudillas remained in prison that morning, and it was not till the afternoon that he was conducted into court. By this time the duumvir was tired and irritable. The *flamen* had arrived and had spoken with Atacinus, and complained that no example had been made, that the Christians were being released, and that, unless some sharp punishments were administered, the people, incensed at the leniency that had been exhibited, would break out in uproar again. Petronius Atacinus, angry, tired out, hungry and peevish, at once sent for the deacon.

The head of the god had been found in his house,

and he had been seen conveying the rescued virgin from the fountain, and must certainly know where she was concealed.

It was noticeable that nothing had been said about the punishing of Æmilius. Even the god, as interpreted by the priestess, had made no demand that he should be dealt with; in fact, had not mentioned him. The duumvir perfectly understood this reticence. Æmilius Lentulus belonged to a good family in the upper town, and to that most powerful and dreaded of all professions—the law. Even the divine founder shrank from attacking a member of the long robe, and a citizen of the upper town.

When Baudillas appeared in court, the magistrate demanded an explanation of the fact of the broken head being found in his house, and further asked of him where Perpetua was concealed.

Baudillas would offer no explanation on the first head; he could not do so without incriminating his brother in the ministry. He denied that he had committed the act of violence, but not that he knew who had perpetrated the outrage. As to where Perpetua was, that he could not say, because he did not know. His profession of ignorance was not believed. He was threatened with torture, but in vain. Thereupon the duumvir sentenced him to be committed to the *robur*, and consigned to the lowest depth thereof, there to remain till such time as he chose to reveal the required information.

Then Petronius Atacinus turned and looked at the *flamen* with a smile, and the latter responded with a well-satisfied nod.

A Roman prison consisted of several parts, and the degree of severity exercised was marked by the portion of the *carcer* to which the prisoner was consigned. Roman law knew nothing of imprisonment for a term as a punishment. The *carcer* was employed either as a place for temporary detention till trial, or else it was one for execution.

The most tolerable portion of the jail consisted of the outer court, with its cells, and a hall for shelter in cold and wet weather. This was in fact the common *atrium* on an enlarged scale and without its luxuries. But there was another part of the prison entitled the *robur*, after the Tullian prison at Rome. This consisted of one large vaulted chamber devoid of window, accessible only by the door, through the interstices of which alone light and air could enter. It derived its name from oak beams planted against the walls, to which were attached chains, by means of which prisoners were fastened to them. In the center of the floor was a round hole, with or without a low breastwork, and this hole communicated with an abyss sometimes given the Greek name of *barathrum*, with conical dome, the opening being in the center. This pit was deep in mire. Into it flowed the sewage of the prison, and the outfall was secured by a grating.* The title of *barathrum* sometimes accorded to this lower portion of the dungeon was derived from a swamp near Athens, in which certain malefactors were smothered.

When Jeremiah was accused before King Zedekiah of inciting the people to come to terms with the Chaldeans, he was put into such a place as this.

"Then took they Jeremiah, and cast him into the dungeon of Malchiah, that was in the court of the prison, and they let down Jeremiah with cords. And in the dungeon there was no water, but mire; so Jeremiah sunk in the mire."

When Paul and Silas were at Philippi, they were imprisoned in the superior portion of the *robur*,

* "Erat et robur, locus in carcere, quo præcipitabatur maleficorum genus, quod ante arcis robustis includebatur."—LIV. 38, 39.

where were the stocks, whereas the other prisoners were in the outer portion, that was more comfortable, and where they had some freedom of movement.

Baudillas turned gray with horror at the thought of being consigned to the awful abyss. His courage failed him and he lost power in his knees, so that he was unable to sustain himself, and the jailer's assistants were constrained to carry him.

As he was conveyed through the outer court, those who were awaiting their trial crowded around him, to clasp and kiss his hand, to encourage him to play the man for Christ, and to salute him reverently as a martyr.

"I am no martyr, good brethren," said the deacon in a feeble voice. "I am not called to suffer for the faith, I have not been asked to sacrifice; I am to be thrown down into the pit, because I cannot reveal what I do not know."

One man, turning to his fellow, said, in a low tone: "If I were given my choice, I would die by fire rather than linger in the pit."

"Will he die there of starvation?" asked another, "or will he smother in the mire?"

"If he be sentenced to be retained there till he

tells what he does not know, he must die there, it matters not how."

"God deliver me from such a trial of my faith! I might win the crown through the sword, but a passage to everlasting life through that foul abyss—that would be past endurance."

As Baudillas was supported through the doorway into the inner prison, he turned his head and looked at the brilliant sky above the yard wall. Then the door was shut and barred behind him. All, however, was not absolutely dark, for there was a gap, through which two fingers could be thrust, under the door, and the sun lay on the threshold and sent a faint reflection through the chamber.

Nevertheless, on entering from the glare of the sun, it seemed to Baudillas at first as though he were plunged in darkness, and it was not for some moments that he could distinguish the ledge that surrounded the well-like opening. The jailer now proceeded to strike a light, and after some trouble and curses, as he grazed his knuckles, he succeeded in kindling a lamp. He now produced a rope, and made a loop at one end about a short crosspole.

"Sit astride on that," said he curtly.

Baudillas complied, and with his hands grasped the cord.

Then slowly he was lowered into the pitch blackness below. Down—down—down he descended, till he plashed into the mire.

The jailer holding the lamp, looked down and called to him to release the rope. The deacon obeyed. There he stood, looking up, watching the dancing pole as it mounted, then saw the spark of the lamp withdrawn; heard the retreating steps of the jailer, then a clash like thunder. The door of the *robur* was shut. He was alone at the bottom of this fetid abyss.

Then he said, and tears coursed down his cheeks as he said it: "Thou hast laid me in the lowest pit—in the place of darkness and in the grave."

CHAPTER XV

"REVEALED UNTO BABES"

On account of the death in the family of the timber merchant, Æmilius left the house and took a room and engaged attendance in the cottage of a cordwainer a little way off. The house was clean, and the good woman was able to cook him a meal not drowned in oil nor rank with garlic.

He was uneasy because Callipodius did not return, and he obtained no tidings concerning Perpetua. The image of this maiden, with a face of transparent purity, out of which shone the radiance of a beautiful soul, haunted his imagination and fluttered his heart. He walked by the side of the flooded tract of land, noticed that the water was falling, and looked, at every turn he took, in the direction of Nemausus, expecting the arrival of his client, but always in vain.

He did at length see a boat approach, towards evening, and he paced the little landing-place with quick strides till it ran up against it; and then only, to his disappointment, did he see that Callipodius was not there. Castor disembarked.

On the strength of his slight acquaintance Æmilius greeted the bishop. The suspense was become unendurable. He asked to be granted a few words in private. To this Castor gladly consented.

He, the head of the Christian community, had remained unmolested. He belonged to a senatorial family in the town, and had relations among the most important officials. The duumvir would undoubtedly leave him alone unless absolutely obliged to lay hands on him. Nemausus was divided into two towns, the Upper and the Lower, each with its own water-supply, its own baths, and each distinct in social composition.

The lower town, the old Gallic city, that venerated the hero-founder of the same name as the town, was occupied by the old Volcian population and by a vast number of emancipated slaves of every nationality, many engaged in trade and very rich. These freedmen were fused into one "order," as it was termed, that of the *Liberti*.

The upper town contained the finest houses, and was inhabited by the Roman colonists, by some descendants of the first Phocean settlers, and by such of the old Gaulish nobility as had most completely identified themselves with their conquerors. These had retained their estates and had enriched themselves by taking Government contracts.

Such scions of the old Gaulish houses had become fused by marriage and community of interest with the families of the first colonists, and they affected contempt for the pure-blooded old aristocracy who had sunk into poverty and insignificance in their decayed mansions in Lower Nemausus.

Of late years, slowly yet surely, the freedmen who had amassed wealth had begun to invade superior Nemausus, had built themselves houses of greater magnificence and maintained an ostentatious splendor that excited the envy and provoked the resentment of the old senatorial and knightly citizens.

The great natural fountain supplied the lower town with water, but was situated at too low a level for the convenience of the gentry of Upper Nemausus, who had therefore conveyed the spring water of Ura from a great distance by tunneling mountains and bridging valleys, and thus had furnished themselves with an unfailing supply of the liquid as necessary to a Roman as was the air he breathed. Thus rendered independent of the natural fountain at the foot of the rocks in Lower Nemausus, those living in the higher town affected the cult of the nymph Ura, and spoke disparagingly of the god of the old town; whereas the inferior part of the city clung tenaciously to the divine Nemausus, whose basin, full of unfailing water, was presented to their very lips and had not to be brought to them from a distance by the engineering skill of men and at a great cost.

Devotion to the god of the fountain in Lower Nemausus was confined entirely to the inhabitants of the old town, and was actually a relic of the old Volcian religion before the advent of the colonists, Greek and Roman. It had maintained itself and its barbarous sacrifice intact, undisturbed.

No victim was exacted from a family of superior Nemausus. The contribution was drawn from among the families of the native nobility, and it was on this account solely that the continuance of the septennial sacrifice had been tolerated.

Already, however, the priesthood was becoming aware that a strong feeling was present that was averse to it. The bulk of the well-to-do population had no traditional reverence for the Gaulish founder-god, and many openly spoke of the devotion of a virgin to death as a rite that deserved to be abolished.

From the cordwainer Æmilius had heard of the mutilation of the statue and of the commotion it had caused. This, he conjectured, accounted for the delay of Callipodius. It had interfered with his action; he had been unable to learn what had become of the damsel, and was waiting till he had definite tidings to bring before he returned. Æmilius was indignant at the wanton act of injury done to a beautiful work of art that decorated one of the loveliest natural scenes in the world. But this indignation was rendered acute by personal feeling. The disturbance caused by the rescue of the virgin might easily have been allayed; not so one provoked by such an act of sacrilege as the defacing of the image of the divine founder. This would exasperate passions and vastly enhance the danger to Perpetua and make her escape more difficult.

As Æmilius walked up from the jetty with the bishop, he inquired of him how matters stood with the Christians in the town and received a general answer. This did not satisfy the young lawyer, and, as the color suffused his face, he asked particularly after Perpetua, daughter of the deceased Harpinius Læto.

The bishop turned and fixed his searching eyes on the young man.

"Why make you this inquiry?" he asked.

"Surely," answered Æmilius, "I may be allowed to feel interest in one whom I was the means of rescuing from death. In sooth, I am vastly concerned to learn that she is safe. It were indeed untoward if she fell once more into the hands of the priesthood or into those of the populace. The ignorant would grip as hard as the interested."

"She is not in the power of either," answered Castor. "But where she is, that God knows, not I. Her mother is distracted, but we trust the maiden has found a refuge among the brethren, and for her security is kept closely concealed. The fewer who know where she is the better will it be, lest torture be employed to extort the secret. The Lady Quincta believes what we have cause to hope and consider probable. This is certain: if she had been discovered and given up to the magistrate the fact would be known at once to all in the place."

"To break the image of the god was a wicked

and a wanton act," said Æmilius irritably. "Is such conduct part of your religion?"

"The act was that of a rash and hot-headed member of our body. It was contrary to my will, done without my knowledge, and opposed to the teaching of our holy fathers, who have ever dissuaded from such acts. But in all bodies of men there are hotheads and impulsive spirits that will not endure control."

"Your own teaching is at fault," said Æmilius peevishly. "You denounce the gods, and yet express regret if one of you put your doctrine in practice."

"If images were ornaments only," said the bishop, "then they would be endurable; but when they receive adoration, when libations are poured at their feet, then we forbid our brethren to take part in such homage, for it is idolatry, a giving to wood and stone the worship due to God alone. But we do not approve of insult offered to any man's religion. No," said Castor emphatically; "Christianity is not another name for brutality, and that is brutality which insults the religious sentiment of the people, who may be ignorant but are sincere."

They had reached the rope-walk. The cordwainer was absent.

"Let us take a turn," said the bishop; and then he halted and smiled and extended his palm to a little child that ran up to him and put its hand within his with innocent confidence.

"This," said Castor, "is the son of the timber merchant." Then to the boy: "Little man, walk with us, but do not interrupt our talk. Speak only when spoken to." He again addressed the lawyer: "My friend, if I may so call thee, thou art vastly distressed at the mutilation of the image. Why so?"

"Because it is a work of art, and that particular statue was the finest example of the sculpture of a native artist. It was a gift to his native town of the god Marcus Antoninus (the Emperor Antoninus Pius)."

"Sir," said Castor, "you are in the right to be incensed. Now tell me this. If the thought of the destruction of a statue made by man and the gift of a Cæsar rouse indignation in your mind, should you not be more moved to see the destruction of living men, as in the shows of the arena—the slaughter of men, the work of God's hands?"

"That is for our entertainment," said Æmilius, yet with hesitation in his voice.

"Does that condone the act of the mutilator of the image, that he did it out of sport, to amuse a few atheists and the vulgar? See you how from his mother's womb the child has been nurtured, how his limbs have grown in suppleness and grace and strength; how his intelligence has developed, how his faculties have expanded. Who made the babe that has become a man? Who protected him from infancy? Who builds up this little tenement of an immortal and bright spirit?" He led forward and indicated the child of Flavillus. "Was it not God? And for a holiday pastime you send men into the arena to be lacerated by wild beasts or butchered by gladiators! Do you not suppose that God, the maker of man, must be incensed at this wanton destruction of His fairest creation?"

"What you say applies to the tree we fell, to the ox and the sheep we slaughter."

"Not so," answered the bishop. "The tree is essential to man. Without it he cannot build himself a house nor construct a ship. The use of the tree is essential to his progress from barbarism. Nay, even in barbarism he requires it to serve him as fuel, and to employ timber demands the fall of the tree. As to the beast, man is so constituted by his Creator that he needs animal food. Therefore is he justified in slaying beasts for his nourishment."

"According to your teaching death sentences are condemned, as also are wars."

"Not so. The criminal may forfeit his right to a life which he is given to enjoy upon condition that he conduce to the welfare of his fellows. If, instead thereof, he be a scourge to mankind, he loses his rights. As to the matter of war: we must guard the civilization we have built up by centuries of hard labor and study after improvement. We must protect our frontiers against the incursions of the barbarians. Unless they be rolled back, they will overwhelm us. Self-preservation is an instinct lodged in every breast, justifying man in defending his life and his acquisitions."

"Your philosophy is humane."

"It is not a philosophy. It is a revelation."

"In what consists the difference?"

"A philosophy is a groping upwards. A revelation is a light falling from above. A philosophy is reached only after the intellect is ripe and experienced, attained to when man's mind is fully developed. A revelation comes to the child as his mind and conscience are opening and shows him his way. Here, little one! stand on that *cippus* and answer me."

Castor took the child in his arms and lifted him to a marble pedestal.

"Little child," said he, "answer me a few simple questions. Who made you?"

"God," answered the boy readily.

"And why did He make you?"

"To love and serve Him."

"And how can you serve Him?"

"By loving all men."

"What did the Great Master say was the law by which we are to direct our lives?"

"'He that loveth God, let him love his brother also.'"

"Little child, what is after death?"

"Eternity."

"And in eternity where will men be?"

"Those that have done good shall be called to life everlasting, and those that have done evil will be cast forth into darkness, where is weeping and gnashing of teeth."

The bishop took the child from the pedestal, and set him again on the ground.

Then, with a smile on his face, he said to Æmilius, "Do we desire to know our way *after* we have erred or *before* we start? What was hidden from the wise and prudent is revealed unto babes. Where philosophy ends, there our religion begins."

CHAPTER XVI

DOUBTS AND DIFFICULTIES

Æmilius paced the rope-walk in deep thought. He did not speak during several turns, and the bishop respected his meditation and kept silence as well.

Presently the young man burst forth with: "This is fairly put, plausible and attractive doctrine. But what we lawyers demand is evidence. When was the revelation made? In the reign of the god Tiberius? That was two centuries ago. What proof is there that this be not a cleverly elaborated philosophy—as you say, a groping upwards—pretending to be, and showing off itself as, a lightening downwards?"

"The evidence is manifold," answered Castor. "In the first place, the sayings and the acts of the Divine Revealer were recorded by evangelists who lived at the time, knew Him, heard Him, or were with those who had daily companied with Him."

"Of what value is such evidence when we cannot put the men who gave it in the witness-box and cross-question them? I do not say that their evidence is naught, but that it is disputable."

"There is other evidence, ever-living, ever-present."

"What is that?"

"Your own reason and conscience. You, Æmilius Lentulus, have these witnesses in yourself. He who made you seated a conscience in your soul to show you that there is such a thing as a law of right and wrong, though, as far as you know, unwritten. Directly I spoke to you of the *sin* of murdering men to make pastime, your color changed; you *knew* that I was right. Your conscience assented to my words."

"I allow that."

"My friend, let me go further. When your mind is not obscured by passion or warped by prejudice, then you perceive that there is a sphere of holiness, of virtue, of purity, to which men have not yet attained, and which, for all you see, is unattainable situated as you are, but one into which, if man could mount, then he would be something nobler than even the poets have conceived. You have flashes of summer lightning in your dark sky. You reject the monstrous fables of the gods as inconsistent with what your reason and conscience tell you comport with divinity. Has any of your gods manifested himself and left such a record of his appearance as is fairly certain? If he appeared, or was fabled to have appeared, did he tell men anything about the nature of God, His will, and the destiny of man? A revelation must be in agreement with the highest aspirations of man. It must be such as will regulate his life, and conduce to his perfection and the advantage of the community. It must be such as will supply him with a motive for rejecting what is base, but pleasing to his coarse nature, and striving after that which is according to the luminous ideal that floats before him. Now the Christian revelation answers these conditions, and is therefore probably true. It supplies man with a reason why he should contend against all that is gross in his nature; should be gentle, courteous, kindly, merciful, pure. It does more. It assures him that the Creator made man in order that he might strive after this ideal, and in so doing attain to serenity and happiness. No other religion that I know of makes such claims; no other professes to have been revealed to man as the law of his being by Him who made man. No other is so completely in accordance on the one hand with what we conceive is in agreement with the nature of God, and on the other so completely accords with our highest aspirations."

"I can say nothing to that. I do not know it."

"Yes, you do know it. The babe declared it; gave you the marrow and kernel of the gospel: Love God and man."

"To fear God is what I can understand; but to love Him is more than I can compass."

"Because you do not know God."

"I do not, indeed."

"God is love."

"A charming sentiment; a rhetorical flourish. What evidence can you adduce that God is love?"

"Creation."

"The earth is full of suffering; violence prevails; wrong overmasters right. There is more of misery than of happiness, saving only to the rich and noble; they are at any rate supposed to be exempt, but, by Hercules, they seem to me to be sick of pleasure, and every delight gluts and leaves a bad taste in the mouth."

"That is true; but why is there all this wretchedness? Because the world is trying to get along without God. Look!" The bishop stooped and took up a green-backed beetle. "If I cast this insect into the water it will suffer and die. If I fling it into the fire it will writhe and perish in agony. Neither water nor fire is the element for which it was created—in which to exist and be happy. The divine law is the atmosphere in which man is made to live. Because there is deflection from that, and man seeks other ends than that for which he was made, therefore comes wretchedness. The law of God is the law man must know, and knowing, pursue to be perfectly happy and to become a perfect being."

"Now I have you!" exclaimed Æmilius, with a laugh. "There are no men more wretched than Christians who possess, and, I presume, keep this law. They abstain from our merry-makings, from the spectacles; they are liable to torture and to death."

"We abstain from nothing that is wholesome and partaken in moderation; but from drunkenness, surfeiting, and what is repugnant to the clean mind. As to the persecution we suffer, the powers of evil rebel against God, and stir up bad men to resist the truth. But let me say something further—if I do not weary you."

"Not at all; you astonish me too much to weary me."

"You are dropped suddenly—cast up by the sea on a strange shore. You find yourself where you have never been before. You know not where to go—how to conduct yourself among the natives; what fruits you may eat as wholesome, and must reject as poisonous. You do not know what course to pursue to reach your home, and fear at every step to get further from it. You cry out for a chart to show you where you are, and in what direction you should direct your steps. Every child born into this world is in a like predicament. It wants a chart, and to know its bearings. This is not the case with any animal. Every bird, fish, beast, knows what to do to fulfill the objects of its existence. Man alone does not. He has aspirations, glimmerings, a law of nature traced, but not filled in. He has lived by that natural law—you live under it, and you experience its inadequacy. That is why your conscience, all mankind, with inarticulate longing desires something further. Now I ask you, as I did once before, is it conceivable that the Creator of man, who put in man's heart that aspiration, that longing to know the law of his being, without which his life is but a miserable shipwreck—is it conceivable that He should withhold from him the chart by which he can find his way?"

"You have given me food for thought. Yet, my doubts still remain."

"I cannot give you faith. That lightens down from above. It is the gift of God. Follow the law of your conscience and He may grant it you. I cannot say when or how, and what means he may employ—but if you are sincere and not a trifler with the truth—He will not deny it you. But see—here comes some one who desires to speak with you."

Æmilius looked in the direction indicated, and saw Callipodius coming up from the water-side, waving his hand to him. So engrossed had he been in conversation with Castor, that he had not observed the arrival of a boat at the landing-place.

At once the young lawyer sped to meet his client, manifesting the utmost impatience.

"What tidings—what news?" was his breathless question.

"As good as may be," answered Callipodius. "The gods work to fulfill thy desire. It is as if thou wert a constraining destiny, or as though it were a pleasure to them to satisfy the wishes of their favorite."

"I pray, lay aside this flattery, and speak plain words."

"Resplendent genius that thou art! thou needest no flattery any more than the sun requires burnishing."

"Let me entreat—the news!"

"In two words——"

"Confine thyself to two words."

"She is safe."

"Where? How?"

"Now must I relax my tongue. In two words I cannot satisfy thy eagerness."

"Then, Body of Bacchus! go on in thine own fashion."

"The account may be crushed into narrow compass. When I left your radiant presence, then I betook myself to the town and found the place in turmoil—the statue of the god had been broken, and the deity was braying like a washerwoman's jackass. The populace was roused and incensed by the outrage, and frightened by the voice of the god. All had quieted down previously, but this worked up the people to a condition of frantic rage and panic.

I hurried about in quest of the Lady Perpetua; and as I learned that she had been conveyed from the pool by Baudillas Macer, I went into the part of the town where he lives; noble once, now slums. Then, lo! thy genius attending and befriending me, whom should I stumble against but a fellow named Tarsius, a slave of a wool merchant to whom I owe moneys, which I haven't yet paid. I knew the fellow from a gash he had received at one time across nose and cheek. He was drunk and angry because he had been expelled the Christian society which was holding its orgies. I warrant thee I frightened the poor wretch with promises of the little horse, the panthers, and the cross, till he became pliant and obliging. Then I wormed out of him all I required, and made him my tool to obtain possession of the pretty maid. I learned from him that the Lady Quincta and her daughter were at the house of Baudillas, afraid to return home because their door was observed by some of the Cultores Nemausi. Then I suborned the rascal to act a part for me. From thy house I dispatched two litters and carriers, and sent that tippling rogue with them to the dwelling of Macer, to say that he was commissioned by his master, Litomarus, to conduct them to his country house for their security. They walked into the snare like fieldfare after juniper berries. Then the porters conveyed the girl to thy house."

"To my house!" Æmilius started.

"Next, she was hurried off as soon as ever the gates were opened, to your villa at Ad Fines."

"And she is there now, with her mother?"

"With her mother! I know better than to do that. I bade the porters convey the old lady in her palanquin to the goose and truffle market and deposit her there. No need to be encumbered with her."

"The Lady Quincta not with her daughter?"

"You were not desirous for further acquaintance with the venerable widow, I presume."

"But," said Æmilius, "this is a grave matter. You have offered, as from me, an insult most wounding to a young lady, and to a respectable matron."

"Generous man! how was it possible for me to understand the niceties that trouble your perspicuous mind? But be at ease. Serious sickness demands strong medicines. Great dangers excuse bold measures. The priestess has demanded the restoration of the virgin. The *flamen Augustalis* is backing her up. So are all the *Seviri*. The religious corporation feel touched in their credit and insist on the restitution. They will heap on fuel, and keep Nemausus in a boil. By no possibility could the damsel have remained hidden in the town. I saw that it was imperiously necessary for me to remove her. I could think of no other place into which to put her than Ad Fines. I managed the matter in admirable fashion; though it is I who say it. But really, by Jupiter Capitolinus, I believe that your genius attended me, and assisted in the execution of the design, which was carried out without a hitch."

Æmilius knitted his arms behind his back, and took short turns, in great perturbation of mind.

"By Hercules!" said he, "you have committed an actionable offense."

"Of course, you look on it from a legal point of view," said Callipodius, a little nettled. "I tell you it was a matter of life or death."

"I do not complain of your having conveyed the young lady to Ad Fines, but of your not having taken her mother there along with her. You have put me in a very awkward predicament."

"How was I to judge that the old woman was to be deported as well?"

"You might have judged that I would cut off my

right hand rather than do aught that might cause people to speak lightly of Perpetua."

The client shrugged his shoulders. "You seem to breed new scruples."

"I thank you," said Æmilius, "that you have shown so good a will, and have been so successful in your enterprise. I am, perhaps, over hasty and exacting. I desired you to do a thing more perfectly than perhaps you were able to perform it. Leave me now. I must clear my mind and discover what is now to be done."

"There is no pleasing some folk," said Callipodius moodily.

CHAPTER XVII

PEDO

Baudillas had been lowered into the pit of the *robur*, and he sank in the slime half-way up his calves. He waded with extended arms, groping for something to which to cling. He knew not whether the bottom were even, or fell into deep holes, into which he might stumble. He knew not whether he were in a narrow well or in a spacious chamber.

Cautiously, in obscurity, he groped, uncertain even whether he went straight or was describing a curve. But presently he touched the wall and immediately discovered a bench, and seated himself thereon. Then he drew up his feet out of the mire, and cast himself in a reclining position on the stone seat.

He looked up, but could not distinguish the opening by which he had been let down into the horrible cess-pit. He was unable to judge to what depth he had been lowered, nor could he estimate the extent of the dungeon in which he was confined.

The bench on which he reposed was slimy, the walls trickled with moisture, were unctuous, and draped with a fungous growth in long folds. The whole place was foul and cold.

How long would his confinement last? Would food, pure water be lowered to him? Or was he condemned to waste away in this pit, from starvation, or in the delirium of famine to roll off from his shelf and smother in the mire?

After a while his eyes became accustomed to the dark and sensitive to the smallest gradations in it; and then he became aware of a feeble glowworm light over the surface of the ooze at one point. Was it that some fungoid growth there was phosphorescent? Or was it that a ray of daylight penetrated there by some tortuous course?

After long consideration it seemed to him probable that the light he distinguished might enter by a series of reflections through the outfall. He thought of examining the opening, but to do so he would be constrained to wade. He postponed the exploration till later. Of one thing he was confident, that although a little sickly light might be able to struggle into this horrible dungeon, yet no means of egress for the person would be left. Precautions against escape by this means would certainly have been taken.

The time passed heavily. At times Baudillas sank into a condition of stupor, then was roused to thought again, again to lapse into a comatose condition. His cut lip was sore, his bruises ached. He had passed his tongue over his broken teeth till they had fretted his tongue raw.

The feeble light at the surface became fainter, and this was finally extinguished. The day was certainly at an end. The sun had set in the west, an auroral glow hung over the place of its decline. Stars were beginning to twinkle; the syringa was pouring forth its fragrance, the flowering thorns their too heavy odor. Dew was falling gently and cool.

The deacon raised his heart to God, and from this terrible pit his prayer mounted to heaven; a prayer not for deliverance from death, but for grace to endure the last trial, and if again put to the test, to withstand temptation. Then he recited the evening prayer of the Church, in Greek: "O God, who art without beginning and without end, the Maker of the world by Thy Christ, and the sustainer thereof, God and Father, Lord of the spirit, King of all things that have reason and life! Thou who hast made the day for the works of light, and the night for the refreshment of our infirmity, for the day is Thine, the night is Thine: Thou hast prepared the light and the sun—do Thou now, O Lord, lover of mankind, fountain of all good, mercifully accept this our evening thanksgiving. Thou who hast brought us through the length of the day, and hast conducted us to the threshold of night, preserve us by Thy Christ, afford us a peaceful evening, and a sinless night, and in the end everlasting life by Thy Christ, through whom be glory, honor and worship in the Holy Spirit, for ever, amen." * After this prayer Baudillas had been wont in the church to say, " Depart in peace! " and to dismiss the faithful. Now he said, "Into Thy hands I commend my spirit."

Out of that fetid abyss and its horrible darkness rose the prayer to God, winged with faith, inspired by fervor sweet with humility, higher than the soaring lark, higher than the faint cloud that caught the last rays of the set sun, higher than the remotest star.

* The prayer is given in the "Apostolic Constitutions," viii. 37.

Presently a confused sound from above reached the prisoner, and a spot of orange light fell on the water below. Then came a voice ringing hollow down the depth, and echoed by the walls, "Thy food!" A slender rope was sent down, to which was attached a basket that contained bread and a pitcher of water. Baudillas stepped into the ooze and took the loaf and the water vessel.

Then the jailer called again: "To-morrow morning—if more be needed—I will bring a second supply. Send up the empty jar when I lower that which is full, if thou art in a condition to require it." He laughed, and the laugh resounded as a bellow in the vaulted chamber.

Few were the words spoken, and they ungracious. Yet was the deacon sensible of pleasure at hearing even a jailer's voice breaking the dreadful silence. He waded back to his ledge, ate the dry bread and drank some of the water. Then he laid himself down again. Again the door clashed, sending thunders below, and once more he was alone.

As his hand traveled along the wall it encountered a hard round knot. He drew his hand away precipitately, but then, moved by curiosity, groped for it again. Then he discovered that this seeming excrescence was a huge snail, there hibernating. He dislodged it, threw it from him and it plashed into the mire.

Time dragged. Not a sound could be heard save the monotonous drip of some leak above. Baudillas counted the falling drops, then wearied of counting, and abandoned the self-imposed task.

Now he heard a far-away rushing sound, then came a blast of hot vapor blowing in his face. He started into a sitting posture, and clung to his bench. In another moment he heard the roar of water that plunged from above; and a hot steam enveloped him. What was the signification of this? Was the pit to be flooded with scalding water and he drowned in it? In a moment he had found the explanation. The water was being let off from the public baths. There would be no more bathers this night. The tide of tepid water rose nearly level with the ledge on which he was crouching, and then ebbed away and rolled forth at the vent through which by day a pale halo had entered.

Half suffocated, part stupefied by the warm vapor, Baudillas sank into a condition without thought, his eyes looking into the blackness above, his ears hearing without noting the dribble from the drain through which the flood had spurted. Presently he was roused by a sense of irritation in every nerve, and putting his hand to his face plucked away some hundred-legged creature, clammy and yet hard, that was creeping over him. It was some time before his tingling nerves recovered. Then gradually torpor stole over him, and he was perhaps unconscious for a couple of hours, when again he was roused by a sharp pain in his finger, and starting, he heard a splash, a rush and squeals. At once he knew that a swarm of rats had invaded the place. He had been bitten by one; his start had disconcerted the creatures momentarily, and they had scampered away.

Baudillas remained motionless, save that he trembled; he was sick at heart. In this awful prison he dared not sleep, lest he should be devoured alive.

Was this to be his end—to be kept awake by horror of the small foes till he could endure the tension no longer, and then sink down in dead weariness and blank indifference on his bench, and at once be assailed from all sides, to feel the teeth, perhaps to attempt an ineffectual battle, then to be overcome and to be picked to his bones?

As he sat still, hardly breathing, he felt the rats again. They were rallying, some swimming, some swarming up on to the shelf. They rushed at him with the audacity given by hunger, with the confidence of experience, and the knowledge of their power when attacking in numbers.

He cried out, beat with his hands, kicked out with his feet, swept his assailants off him by the score; yet such as could clung to his garment by their teeth and, not discomfited, quickly returned. To escape them he leaped into the mire; he plunged this way, then that; he returned to the wall; he attempted to scramble up it beyond their reach, but in vain.

Wherever he went, they swam after him. He was unarmed, he could kill none of his assailants; if he could but decimate the horde it would be something. Then he remembered the pitcher and felt for that. By this time he had lost his bearings wholly. He knew not where he had left the vessel. But by creeping round the circumference of his prison, he must eventually reach the spot where he had previously been seated, and with the earthenware vessel he would defend himself as long as he was able.

Whilst thus wading, he was aware of a cold draught blowing in his face, and he knew that he had reached the opening of the sewer that served as outfall. He stooped and touched stout iron bars forming part of a grating. He tested them, and assured himself that they were so thick set that it was not possible for him to thrust even his head between them.

All at once the rats ceased to molest him. They had retreated, whither he could not guess, and he knew as little why. Possibly, they were shrewd enough to know that they had but to exercise patience, and he must inevitably fall a prey to their teeth.

Almost immediately, however, he was aware of a little glow, like that of a spark, and of a sound of splashing. He was too frightened, too giddy, to collect his thoughts, so as to discover whence the light proceeded, and what produced the noise.

Clinging to the grating, Baudillas gazed stupidly at the light, that grew in brightness, and presently irradiated a face. This he saw, but he was uncertain whether he actually did see, or whether he were a prey to an illusion.

Then the light flashed over him, and his eyes after

a moment recognized the face of his old slave, Pedo. A hand on the further side grasped one of the stanchions, and the deacon heard the question, "Master, are you safe?"

"Oh, Pedo, how have you come into this place?"

"Hush, master. Speak only in a whisper. I have waded up the sewer (*cloaca*), and have brought with me two stout files. Take this one, and work at the bar on thy side. I will rasp on the other. In time we shall cut through the iron, and then thou wilt be able to escape. When I heard whither thou hadst been cast, then I saw my way to making an effort to save thee."

"Pedo! I will give thee thy liberty!"

"Master! it is I who must first manumit thee."

Then the slave began to file, and as he filed he muttered, "What is liberty to me? At one time, indeed! Ah, at one time, when I was young, and so was Blanda! But now I am old and lame. I am well treated by a good master. Well, well! Sir! work at the bar where I indicate with my finger. That is a transversal stanchion and sustains the others."

Hope of life returned. The heart of Baudillas

was no longer chilled with fear and his brain stunned with despair. He worked hard, animated by eagerness to escape. There was a spring of energy in the little flame of the lamp, an inspiring force in the presence of his slave. The bar was thick, but happily the moisture of the place and the sour exhalations had corroded it, so that thick flakes of rust fell off under the tool.

"Yesterday, nothing could have been done for you, sir," said Pedo, "for the inundation was so extensive that the sewer was closed with water that had risen a foot above the opening into the river. But, thanks be to God, the flood has fallen. Those who know the sky declare that we shall have a blast of the *circius* (the mistral) on us suddenly, and bitter weather. The early heat has dissolved the snows over-rapidly and sent the water inundating all the low land. Now with cold, the snows will not melt."

"Pedo," said the deacon, "hadst thou not come, the rats would have devoured me. They hunted me as a pack of wolves pursue a deer in the Cebennæ."

"I heard them, master, as I came up the sewer. There are legions of them. But they fear the light, and as long as the lamp burns will keep their distance."

"Pedo," whispered Baudillas again, after a pause, whilst both worked at the bar. "I know not how it was that when I stood before the duumvir, I did not betray my Heavenly Master. I was so frightened. I was as in a dream. They may have thought me firm, but I was in reality very weak. Another moment, or one more turn of the rack and I would have fallen."

"Master! God's strength is made perfect in weakness."

"Yes, it is so. I myself am a poor nothing. Oh, that I had the manhood of Marcianus!"

"Press against the bar, master. With a little force it will yield."

Pedo removed the lamp that he had suspended by a hook from the crossbar. Baudillas threw himself with his full weight against the grating, and the stanchion did actually snap under the impact, at the place where filed.

"That is well," said the slave. "Thy side of the bar is also nearly rasped through. Then we must saw across this upright staff of iron. To my thinking it is not fastened below."

"It is not. I have thrust my foot between it and the paving. Methinks it ends in a spike and barbs."

"If it please God that we remove the grating, then thou must follow me, bending low."

"Is the distance great?"

"Sixty-four paces of thine; of mine, more, as I do but hobble."

"Hah! this is ill-luck."

With the energy of filing, and owing to the loosened condition of the bar, the lamp had been displaced, and it fell from where it had been suspended and was extinguished in the water.

Both were now plunged in darkness as of Erebus, and were moreover exposed to danger from the rats. But perhaps the grating of the files, or the whispers of the one man to the other, alarmed the suspicious beasts, and they did not venture to approach.

"Press, master! I will pull," said the slave. His voice quivered with excitement.

Baudillas applied his shoulder to the grating, and Pedo jerked at it sharply.

With a crack it yielded; with a plash it fell into the water.

"Quick, my master—lay hold of my belt and

follow. Bow your head low or you will strike the roof. We must get forth as speedily as may be."

"Pedo! the jailer said that if alive I was to give a sign on the morrow. He believes that during the night I will be devoured by rats, as doubtless have been others."

"Those executed in the prison are cast down there."

"Perhaps," said Baudillas, "if he meet with no response in the morning he will conclude that I am dead, and I do not think he will care to descend and discover whether it be so."

After a short course through the arched passage, both stood upright; they were to their breasts in water, but the water was fresh and pure. Above their heads was the vault of heaven, not now spangled with stars but crossed by scudding drifts of vapor.

Both men scrambled out of the river to the bank, and then Baudillas extended his arms, and said, with face turned to the sky:

"I waited patiently for the Lord, and He inclined unto me, and heard my calling. He hath brought me also out of the horrible pit, out of the mire and clay, and hath set my feet upon the rock. And He hath put a new song in my mouth, even a thanksgiving unto our God." *

* The casting into the lowest pit of the *robur*—sometimes termed the *barathrum*—was not a rare act of barbarity. Jugurtha perished in that of the Tullianum in Rome. "By Hercules!" said he as he was being lowered into it, "your bath is cold!" S. Ferreolus, of Vienne, was plunged into this horrible place in A.D. 304. He was young, and by diving or by working at the grating he managed to escape much in the manner described above. Thus through the sewer he reached the Rhône, and swam across it. He was, however, recaptured and taken back to Vienne, where he was decapitated. He is commemorated in the diocese of Vienne on September 18th, and is mentioned by Sidonius Apollinaris in the fifth century, and by Venantius Fortunatus in the sixth. S. Gregory, the illuminator, was cast into the *barathrum* by Tiridates. Theodoret describes martyrs devoured by rats and mice in Persia ("Hist. Eccl.," v. 39).

CHAPTER XVIII

IN THE CITRON-HOUSE

Perpetua, at Ad Fines, was a prey to unrest. She was in alarm for the safety of her mother, and she was disconcerted at having been smuggled off to the house of a man who was a stranger, though to him she owed her life.

The villa was in a lovely situation, with a wide outstretch of landscape before it to the Rhône, and beyond to the blue and cloudlike spurs of the Alps; and the garden was in the freshness of its first spring beauty. But she was in too great trouble to concern herself about scenery and flowers. Her thoughts turned incessantly to her mother. In the embarrassing situation in which she was—and one that was liable to become far more embarrassing—she needed the support and counsel of her mother.

Far rather would she have been in prison at Nemausus, awaiting a hearing before the magistrate, and perhaps condemnation to death, than be as at present in a charming country house, attended by obsequious servants, provided with every comfort, yet ignorant why she had been brought there, and what the trials were to which she would be subjected.

The weather had changed with a suddenness not infrequent in the province. The warm days were succeeded by some of raging wind and icy rains. In fact, the mistral had begun to blow. As the heated air rose from the stony plains, its place was supplied by that which was cold from the snowy surfaces of the Alps, and the downrush was like that to which we nowadays give the term of blizzard. So violent is the blast on these occasions that the tillers of the soil have to hedge round their fields with funereal cypresses, to form a living screen against a wind that was said, or fabled, to have blown the cow out of one pasture into that of another farmer, but which, without fable, was known to upset ricks and carry away the roofs of houses.

To a cloudless sky, traversed by a sun of almost summer brilliancy, succeeded a heaven dark, iron-gray, with whirling vapors that had no contour, and which hung low, trailing their dripping skirts over the shivering landscape.

Trees clashed their boughs. The wood behind the villa roared like a cataract. In the split ledges and prongs of limestone, among the box bushes and junipers, the wind hissed and screamed. Birds fled for refuge to the eaves of houses or to holes in the cliffs. Cattle were brought under shelter. Sheep crouched dense packed on the lee side of a stone wall. The very ponds and lagoons were whipped and their surfaces flayed by the blast. Stones were dislodged on the mountain slopes, and flung down; pebbles rolled along the plains, as though lashed forward by whips. The penetrating cold necessitated the closing of every shutter, and the heating of the hypocaust under the house. In towns, in the houses of the better classes, the windows were glazed with thin flakes of mica (*lapis specularis*), a transparent stone brought from Spain and Cappadocia, but in the country this costly luxury was dispensed with, as the villas were occupied only in the heat of summer, when there was no need to exclude the air. The window openings were closed with shutters. Rooms were not warmed by fireplaces, with wood fires on hearths, but by an arrangement beneath the mosaic and cement floor, where a furnace was kindled, and the smoke and heated air were carried by numerous pipes up the walls on all sides, thus producing a summer heat within when all was winter without.

In the fever of her mind, Perpetua neither felt

the asperity of the weather nor noticed the comfort of the heated rooms. She was incessantly restless, was ever running to the window or the door, as often to be disappointed, in anticipation of meeting her mother. She was perplexed as to the purpose for which she had been conveyed to Ad Fines. The slave woman, Blanda, who attended her, was unable or unwilling to give her information. All she pretended to know was that orders had been issued by Callipodius, friend and client of Æmilius Lentulus, her master, that the young lady was to be made comfortable, was to be supplied with whatever she required, and was on no account to be suffered to leave the grounds. The family was strictly enjoined not to mention to any one her presence in the villa, under pain of severe chastisement.

Blanda was kind and considerate, and had less of the fawning dog in her manner than was customary among slaves. It was never possible, even for masters, to trust the word of their servants; consequently Perpetua, who knew what slaves were, placed little reliance on the asseverations of ignorance that fell from the lips of Blanda. There was, in the conversation of Blanda, that which the woman intended to reassure, but which actually heightened the uneasiness of the girl—this was the way in which the woman harped continually on the good looks, amiability and wealth of her master, who, as she insisted, belonged to the Voltinian tribe, and was therefore one of the best connected and highest placed in the colony.

The knowledge that she had been removed to Ad Fines to insure her safety did not satisfy Perpetua; and she was by no means assured that she had thus been carried off with the approbation and knowledge of her mother, or of the bishop and principal Christians of her acquaintance in Nemausus. Of Æmilius Varo she really knew nothing save that he was a man of pleasure and a lawyer.

Adjoining the house was a conservatory. Citron trees and oleanders in large green-painted boxes were employed in summer to decorate the terrace and gardens. They were allowed to be out in mild winters, but directly the mistral began to howl, the men-servants of the house had hurriedly conveyed them within doors into the conservatory, as the gale would strip them of their fruit, bruise the leaves and injure the flowers.

In her trouble of mind, unable to go abroad in the bitter weather, impatient of quiet, Perpetua entered the citron-house and walked among the trees in their green tubs, now praying for help, then wiping the drops from her eyes and brow.

As she thus paced, she heard a stir in the house, the opening of doors, the rush of wind driving through it, the banging of valves and rattle of shutters. Then she heard voices, and among them one that was imperious. A moment later, Blanda ran to Perpetua, and after making a low obeisance said: "The master is come. He desires permission to speak with you, lady, when he hath had his bath and hath assumed a change of raiment. For by the mother goddesses, no one can be many moments without and not be drenched to the bone. And this exhibits the master's regard for thee, lady; his extreme devotion to your person and regard for your comfort, that he has exposed himself to cold and rain and wind so as to come hither to inquire if you are well, and if there be aught you desire that he can perform to content you."

What was Perpetua to do? She plucked some citron blossoms in her nervous agitation, unknowing what she did, then answered timidly: "I am in the house of the noble Æmilius. Let him speak with me here when it suits his convenience. Yet stay,

14

Blanda! Inquire at once, whether he brings me tidings of my dear mother."

The slave hasted away, and returned directly to inform Perpetua that her master was grieved to relate that he was unable to give her the desired information, but that he only awaited instructions from Perpetua to take measures to satisfy her.

Then the girl was left alone, and in greater agitation than before. She walked among the evergreens, putting the citron flowers to her nose, plucking off the leaves, pressing her hand to her brow, and wiping her distilling eyes.

The conservatory was unglazed. It was furnished with shutters in which were small openings like those in fiddles. Consequently a twilight reigned in the place; what light entered was colorless, and without brilliancy. Through the openings could be seen the whirling vapors; through them also the rain spluttered in, and the wind sighed a plaintive strain, now and then rising to a scream.

Perpetua still held the little bunch of citron in her hand; she was as unaware that she held it as that she had plucked it. Her mind was otherwise engaged, and her nervous fingers must needs clasp something.

As she thus walked, fearing the appearance of Æmilius, and yet desirous of having a term put to her suspense, she heard steps, and in another moment the young lawyer stood before her. He bowed with hands extended, and with courtly consideration would not draw near. Aware that she was shy or frightened, he said: " I have to ask your pardon, young lady, for this intrusion on your privacy, above all for your abduction to this house of mine. It was done without my having been consulted, but was done with good intent, by a friend, to place you out of danger. I had no part in the matter; nevertheless I rejoice that my house has had the honor of serving you as a refuge from such as seek your destruction."

" I thank you," answered the girl constrainedly. " I owe you a word of acknowledgment of my lively gratitude for having rescued me from the fountain, and another for affording me shelter here. But if I may be allowed to ask a favor, it is that my mother be restored to me, or me to my mother."

" Alas, lady," said Æmilius, " I have no knowledge where she is. I myself have been in concealment—for the rabble has been incensed against me for what I was privileged to do, at the Nemausean basin, unworthy that I was. I have not since ventured into the town; not that I believe the rabble would dare attempt violence against me, but I do not think it wise to allow them the chance. I sent my good, blundering friend Callipodius to inquire what had become of you, as I was anxious lest you should again be in peril of your life; and he—Callipodius—seeing what a ferment there was in the town, and how determined the priesthood was to get you once more into its power, he consulted his mother wit, and had you conveyed to my country house. Believe me, lady, he was actuated by a sincere wish to do you service. If he had but taken the Lady Quincta away as well, and lodged her here along with you, I would not have a word of reproach for him, nor entertain a feeling of guilt in your eyes."

"My mother was in the first litter."

"That litter did not pass out of the gates of Nemausus. Callipodius was concerned for your safety, as he knew that it was you who were menaced and not your mother."

"But it is painful for me to be away from my mother."

"Lady! you are safer separated from her. If she

be, as I presume, still in the town, then those who pursue you will prowl about where she is, little supposing that you are elsewhere, and the secret of your hiding-place cannot be wrung from her if she does not herself know it."

"I concern myself little about my life," said Perpetua. "But, to be alone here, away from her, from every relation, in a strange house——"

"I know what you would say, or rather what you feel and do not like to say. I have a proposal to make to you which will relieve your difficulty if it commends itself to you. It will secure your union with your mother, and prevent anything being spoken as to your having been concealed here that may offend your honorable feelings."

Perpetua said nothing. She plucked at the petals of the citron flower and strewed them on the marble pavement.

"You have been brought to this house, and happily none know that you are here, save my client, Callipodius, and myself. But what I desire to say is this. Give me a right to make this your refuge, and me a right to protect you. If I be not distasteful to you, permit this. I place myself unreservedly in your hands. I love you, but my respect for you equals my love. I am rich and enjoy a good position. I have nothing I can wish for but to be authorized by you to be your defender against every enemy. Be my wife, and not all the fools and *flamines* of the province can touch a hair of your head."

The tears welled into Perpetua's eyes. She looked at the young man, who stood before her with such dignity and gentleness of demeanor. He seemed to her to be as noble, as good as a heathen well could be. He felt for her delicate position; he had risked his life and fortunes to save her. He had roused the powerful religious faction of his native city against him, and he was now extending his protection over her against the priesthood and the mob of Nemausus.

"I know," pursued Æmilius, "that I am not worthy of one such as yourself. I offer myself because I see no other certain means of making you secure, save by your suffering me to be your legitimate defender. If your mother will consent, and I am so happy as to have yours, then we will hurry on the rites which shall make us one, and not a tongue can stir against you and not a hand be lifted to pluck you from my side."

Perpetua dropped the flower, now petalless. She

could not speak. He respected her emotions, and continued to address her.

"I am confident that I can appease the excitement among the people and the priests, and those attached to the worship of the divine ancestor. They will not dare to push matters to extremities. The sacrifice has been illegal all along, but winked at by the magistrates because a custom handed down with the sanction of antiquity. But a resolute protest made—if need be an appeal to Cæsar—and the priesthood are paralyzed. Consider also that as my wife they could no longer demand you. Their hold on you would be done for, as none but an unmarried maid may be sacrificed. The very utmost they can require in their anger and disappointment will be that you should publicly sprinkle a few grains of incense on the altar of Nemausus."

"I cannot do that. I am a Christian."

"Believe what you will. Laugh at the gods as do I and many another. A few crumbs of frankincense, a little puff of smoke that is soon sped."

"It may not be."

"Remain a Christian, adhere to its philosophy or revelation, as Castor calls it. Attend its orgies, and be the protectress of your fellow-believers."

"None the less, I cannot do it."

"But why not?"

"I cannot be false to Christ."

"What falsehood is there in this?"

"It is a denial of Him."

"Bah! He died two hundred years ago."

"He lives, He is ever present, He sees and knows all."

"Well, then He will not look harshly on a girl who acts thus to save her life."

"I should be false to myself as well as to Him."

"I cannot understand this——"

"No, because you do not know and love Him."

"Love Him!" echoed Æmilius, "He is dead. You never saw Him at any time. It is impossible for any one to love one invisible, unseen, a mere historical character. See, we have all over Gallia Narbonensis thousands of Augustals; they form a sect, if you will. All their worship is of Augustus Cæsar, who died before your Christ. Do you suppose that one among those thousands loves him whom they worship, and after whom they are named, and who is their bond of connection? No —it is impossible. It cannot be."

"But with us, to know is to love. Christ is the

power of God, and we love Him because He first loved us."

"Riddles, riddles!" said Æmilius, shaking his head.

"It is a riddle that may be solved to you some day. I would give my life that it were."

"You would?"

"Aye, and with joy. You risked your life for me. I would give mine to win for you——"

"What?"

"Faith. Having that you would know how to love."

CHAPTER XIX

MARCIANUS

When the deacon Baudillas and his faithful Pedo emerged from the river, and stood on the bank, they were aware how icy was the blast that blew, for it pierced their sodden garments and froze the marrow in their bones.

"Master," said Pedo, "this is the beginning of a storm that will last for a week; you must get under shelter, and I will give you certain garments I have provided and have concealed hard by in a kiln. The gates of the town are shut. I have no need to inform you that we are without the city walls."

Pedo guided the deacon to the place where he had hidden a bundle of garments, and which was not a bowshot distant from the mouth of the sewer. The kiln was small; it had happily been in recent use, for it was still warm, and the radiation was grateful to Baudillas, whose teeth were chattering in his head.

"I have put here bread and meat, and a small skin of wine," said the slave. "I advise you, master, to make a meal; you will relish your food better here than in the black-hole. Whilst we eat we consume time likewise; but the dawn is returning, and with it the gates will be opened and we shall slip in among the market people. But, tell me, whither will you go?"

"I would desire, were it advisable, to revisit my own house," said the deacon doubtfully.

"And I would advise you to keep clear of it," said the slave. "Should the jailer discover that you have escaped, then at once search will be made for you, and, to a certainty it will begin at your habitation." Then, with a dry laugh, he added, "And if it be found that I have assisted in your evasion, then there will be one more likely to give sport to the people at the forthcoming show. Grant me the wild beasts and not the cross."

"I will not bring thee into danger, faithful friend."

"I cannot run away on my lame legs," said Pedo. "Ah! as to those shows. They are to wind up with a water-fight—such is the announcement. There will be gladiators from Arelate sent over to contend in boats against a fleet of our Nemausean ruffians. On the previous day there will be sport with wild beasts. I am told that there have been wolves trapped during the winter in the Cebennæ, and sent down here, where they are retained fasting. I have heard their howls at night and they have disturbed my sleep—their howls and the aches in my thigh. I knew the weather would change by the pains in my joint. There is a man named Amphilochius, a manumitted slave, who broke into and robbed the villa of the master who had freed him. He is a Greek of Iconium, and the public are promised that he shall be cast to the beasts; but whether to the panthers, or the wolves, or bear, or given to be gored by a bull, that I know not. Then there is a taverner from somewhere on the way to Ugernum, who for years has murdered such of his guests as he esteemed well furnished with money, and has thrown their carcasses into the river. He will fight the beasts. There is a bear from Larsacus; but they tell me he is dull, has not yet shaken off his winter sleep, and the people fear they will get small entertainment out of him."

"You speak of these scenes with relish."

"Ah! master, before I was regenerate I dearly loved the spectacles. But the contest with bulls! That discovers the agility of a man. Falerius

Volupius Servilianus placed rosettes between their horns and gave a prize to any who would pluck them away. That was open to be contested for by all the youths of Nemausus. There was little danger to life or limb, and it taught them to be quick of eye and nimble in movement. But it was because none were gored that the spectators wearied of these innocent sports and clamored for the butchery of criminals and the contests of gladiators. There was a fine Numidian lion brought by a shipmaster to Agatha; a big price was asked, and the citizens of Narbo outbid us, so we lost that fine fellow."

"Ah, Pedo! please God that none of the brethren be exposed to the beasts."

"I think there will not be many. The Quatuor-viri are slow to condemn, and Petronius Atacinus most unwilling of all. There are real criminals in the prison sufficient to satisfy an ordinary appetite for blood. But, see! we are discussing the amphitheater and not considering whither thou wilt betake thyself."

"I have been turning the matter over, and I think that I will go first to Marcianus, my brother-deacon, and report myself to be alive and free, that he may inform the bishop; and I will take his advice as to my future conduct, and where I shall bestow myself."

"He has remained unmolested," said the slave, "and that is to me passing strange, for I have been told that certain of the brethren, when questioned relative to the mutilation of the statue, have accused him by name. Yet, so far, nothing has been done. Yet I think his house is watched; I have noticed one Burrhus hanging about it; and Tarsius, they say, has turned informer. See, master! the darkness is passing away; already there is a wan light in the east."

"Had the mouth of the kiln been turned to the setting in place of the rising sun, we should not have felt the wind so greatly. Well, Pedo, we will be on the move. Market people from the country will be at the gates. I will consult with Marcianus before I do aught."

An hour later, Baudillas and his attendant were at the gate of Augustus, and passed in unchallenged. Owing to the furious mistral, accompanied by driving rain, the guards muffled themselves in their cloaks and paid little attention to the peasants bringing in their poultry, fish and vegetables for sale. The deacon and his slave entered unnoticed along with a party of these. In the street leading to the forum was a knot of people about an angry potter whose stall had been blown over by the wind. He had set boards on trestles, and laid out basins, pitchers, lamps, urns on the planks; over all he had stretched sail-cloth. The wind had caught the awning and beaten it down, upsetting and crushing his ware. The potter was swearing that he was ruined, and that his disaster was due to the Christians, who had exasperated the gods by their crimes and impieties.

Some looking on laughed and asked, shouting, whether the gods did not blow as strong blasts out of their lungs every year about the same time, and whether they did so because annually insulted.

"But they don't break my crocks," stormed the potter.

"Charge double for what remain unfractured," joked an onlooker.

"Come, master," said Pedo, plucking Baudillas by the sleeve. "If that angry fellow recognize you, you are lost. Hold my cloak and turn down the lane, then we are at the *posticum*, at the back of the house. I know some of the family, and they will admit us."

Near by was a shop for flowers. Over the shop front was the inscription, "Non vendo nisi amantibus coronas" ("I sell garlands to lovers only").* The woman in charge of the bunches and crowns of spring flowers looked questioningly at Baudillas. Her wares were such as invited only when the sun shone. The poor flowers had a draggled and desponding appearance. No lovers came to buy in the bitter mistral.

"Come, master, we shall be recognized," said Pedo.

In another moment they had passed out of the huffle of the wind and the drift of the rain into the shelter and warmth of a dwelling.

Pedo bade a slave go to Marcianus and tell the deacon that someone below desired a word with him. Almost immediately the man returned with orders to conduct the visitor to the presence of the master.

Baudillas was led along a narrow passage into a chamber in the inner part of the house, away from the apartments for the reception of guests.

The room was warmed. It was small, and had a glazed window; that is to say, the opening was closed

* This sign is now in the museum.

by a sheet of stalagmite from one of the caves of Larsacus, cut thin.

In this chamber, seated on an easy couch, with a roll in his hand, which he was studying, was Marcianus. His countenance was hard and haughty.

"You!" he exclaimed, starting with surprise. "What brings you here? I heard that you had been before the magistrate and had confessed. But, bah! of such as you martyrs are not made. You have betrayed us and got off clear yourself."

"You mistake, brother," answered Baudillas, modestly. "In one thing are you right—I am not of the stuff out of which martyrs and confessors are fashioned. But I betrayed no one. Not that there is any merit due to me for that. I was in such a dire and paralyzing fright that I could not speak."

"How then come you here?"

"As we read that the Lord sent His angel to deliver Peter from prison, so has it been with me."

"You lie!" said Marcianus angrily. "No miracle was wrought for you—for such as you who shiver and quake and lose power of speech! Bah! Come, give me a more rational explanation of your escape."

"My slave was the angel who delivered me."

"So you ran away! Could not endure martyr-

15

dom, saw the crown shining, and turned tail and used your legs. I can well believe it. Coward! Unworthy of the name of a Christian, undeserving of the cross marked on thy brow, unbecoming of the ministry."

"I know that surely enough," said Baudillas; "I am of timorous stuff, and from childhood feared pain. But I have not denied Christ."

"What has brought you here?" asked Marcianus curtly.

"I have come to thee for counsel."

"The counsel I give thou wilt not take. What saith the Scripture: 'He that putteth his hand to the plough and turneth back is not fit for the kingdom of God.' Thou wast called to a glorious confession, and looked back and ran away."

"And thy counsel?"

"Return and surrender, and win the crown and palm. But it is waste of breath to say such words to thee. I know thee. Wast thou subjected to torture?"

"No, brother."

"No; not the rack, nor the torches, nor the hooks, nor the thumbscrews. Oh, none of these!"

"No, brother. It is true, I was scarce tried at

all. Indeed, it was good luck—God forgive me!—it was through His mercy that I was saved from denying the faith. I was not even asked to sacrifice."

"Well; go thy ways. I cannot advise thee."

"Stay," said Baudillas. "I saw in the outer prison some of the faithful, but was in too great fear to recognize any. Who have been taken?"

"The last secured has been the widow Quincta. The pontiff and the *flamen* Augustalis and the priestess of Nemausus swear that she shall be put on the rack and tortured till she reveals where her daughter is concealed, and that amiable drone, the acting magistrate, has given consent. Dost thou know where the damsel Perpetua is concealed?"

"Indeed, Marcianus, I know not. But tell me: hast thou not been inquired for? I have been told how that some have accused thee."

"Me! Who said that?"

Marcianus started, and his face worked. "Bah! they dare not touch me. I belong to the Falerii; we have had magistrates in our family, and one clothed with the pro-consulship. They will not venture to lay hands on me."

"But what if they know, and it is known through

the town, that it was thou who didst mutilate the statue of the founder?"

"They do not know it."

"Nay, thou deceivest thyself. It is known. Some of those who were at the Agape have spoken."

"It was thou—dog that thou art!"

"Nay, it was not I."

Marcianus rose and strode up and down the room, biting his nails. Then, contemptuously, he said: "My family will stand between me and mob or magistrate. I fear not. But get thee gone. Thou compromisest me by thy presence, thou runagate and jail-breaker."

"I came here but to notify my escape and to ask counsel of thee."

"Get thee gone. Fly out of Nemausus, or thy chattering tongue will be set going and reveal everything that ought to be kept secret." Then taking a turn he added to himself, "I belong to the Falerii."

Baudillas left; and, as he went from the door, Pedo whispered in his ear: "Let us escape to Ad Fines. We can do so in this detestable weather. I have an old friend there, named Blanda. In my youth I loved—ah! welladay! that was long ago—and we were the chattels of different masters, so it came to naught. She is still a slave, but she may be able to assist us. I can be sure of that; for the remembrance of our old affection, she will do what lies in her power to secrete us."

He suddenly checked himself, plucked the deacon back, and drew him against the wall.

An ædile, attended by a body of the city police, armed like soldiers, advanced and silently surrounded the house of Marcianus.

Then the officer struck the door thrice, and called: "By the authority of Petronius Atacinus and Vibius Fuscianus, Quatuor-viri juridicundo, and in the name of the Imperator Cæsar Augustus, Marcus Aurelius Antoninus, I arrest Cneius Falerius Marcianus, on the atrocious charge of sacrilege."

CHAPTER XX

IN THE BASILICA

The Quatuorvir Petronius Atacinus, who was on duty, occupied his chair in the stately Plotinian Basilica, or court of justice, that had been erected by Hadrian, in honor of the lady to whose ingenious and unscrupulous maneuvers he owed his elevation to the throne of the Cæsars. Of this magnificent structure nothing remains at present save some scraps of the frieze in the museum.

When the weather permitted, Petronius or his colleagues liked to hear a case in the open air, from a tribune in the forum. But this was impossible to-day, in the howling wind and lashing rain. The court itself was comparatively deserted. A very few had assembled to hear the trials. None who had a warmed home that day left it uncalled for. Some market women set their baskets in the doorway and stepped inside, but it was rather because they were wet and out of breath than because they were interested in the proceedings. Beside the magistrate sat the chief *pontifex* who was also Augustal *flamen*.

Of *pontifices* there were three in the city, but one of these was a woman, the priestess of Nemausus.

Throughout the south of Gaul the worship of Augustus had become predominant, and had displaced most of the ancestral cults. The temples dedicated to Augustus exceeded in richness all others, and were crowded when the rest were deserted.

Jupiter was only not forgotten because he had borrowed some of the attributes of the Gallic solar deity, and he flourished the golden wheel in one hand and brandished the lightnings in the other. Juno had lent her name to a whole series of familiar spirits of the mountains and of the household, closely allied to the *Proxumes*, a set of domestic Brownies or Kobolds, who were chiefly adored and propitiated by the women, and who had no other temple than the hearth. At Tarasconum, the Phœnician goddess Britomartis reigned supreme, and her worship was stimulated by a grand annual procession and dramatic representation of her conquest over a dragon. At Nemausus the corresponding god of war was called Mars Britovius. But the Volcæ Arecomici were a peaceably-disposed people, and paid little devotion to the god of battles. The cult of the founder Nemausus did not flag, but that of Augustus was in the ascendant. All the freedmen were united in one great sodality under his invocation, and this guild represented an important political factor in the land. It had its religious officers, its *flamines* and *seviri*, attended by lictors, and the latter had charge of all the altars at the crossroads, and sat next to the civic functionaries in the courts, at banquets, in the theater. Rich citizens bequeathed large sums to the town and to the sodalities to be expended in public feasts, in largesses, and in gladiatorial shows. The charge of these bequests, as also their distribution, was in the hands of the *flamines* and *seviri*. The priesthood was, therefore, provided with the most powerful of all means for gaining and moving the multitude, which desired nothing better than bread and games.

"Have that door shut!" called the magistrate. "It bangs in this evil wind, and I cannot even hear what my excellent friend Lucius Smerius is saying in my ear; how then can I catch what is said in court?" Then, turning to the pontiff, he said: "I detest this weather. Last year, about this time, I was struck with an evil blast, and lost all sense of smell and taste for nine months. I had pains in my loins and an ache in all my bones. I doubt if even the jests of Baubo could have made me laugh; I was in lower dumps than even Ceres. Even now, when seated far too long in this marble chair, I get an ache across my back that assures me I am no longer young. But I could endure that if my sense of taste had been fully restored. I do not relish good wine as of old, and that is piteous, and I really at times think of suicide."

"It was the work of enchantment," said the pontiff. "These Christians, in their orgies, stick pins into images to produce pains in those the figures represent."

"How do you know this? Have you been initiated into their mysteries?"

"I——! The Immortals preserve me therefrom."

"Then, by Pluto, you speak what you have heard of the gossips—old wives' babble. I will tell you what my opinion is, Smerius. If you were to thrust your nose into the mysteries of the Bona Dea you would find—what? No more than did Clodius— nothing at all. My wife, she attends them, and comes home with her noddle full of all the tittle-tattle of Nemausus. It is so with the Christian orgies. I would not give a snap of the fingers for all the secrets confided to the initiated—neither in Eleusis nor in the Serapium, nor among the Christians."

"These men are not like others; they are unsociable, brutish, arrogant."

"Unsociable I allow. Brutish! The word is inapt; for, on the contrary, I find them very simple, soft-headed, pulp-hearted folk. They abstain from all that is boisterous and cruel. Arrogant they may be. There I am at one with you. 'Live and let live' is my maxim. We have a score of gods, home made and foreign, and they all rub and tumble together without squabbling. Of late we have had Madame Isis over from Egypt, and the White Ladies,* and the Proxumes, Victoria Augusta, Venus, and Minerva, make room for her without even a frown on their divine faces. And imperial Rome sanctions all these devotions. Why, did not the god Augustus build a temple here to Nemausus and pay him divine honors, though he had never heard him named before? Now this Christian sect is exclusive. It will suffer no gods to stand beside Him whom they adore. He must reign alone.

* Fairies, adored at Nemausus.

That I call illiberal, narrow-minded, against the spirit of the age and the principle of Roman policy. That is the reason why I dislike these Christians."

"Here come the prisoners. My good friend, do not be too easy with them. It will not do. The temper of the people is up. The sodality of Augustus swear that they will not decree you a statue, and will oppose your nomination to the knighthood. They have joined hands with the Cultores Nemausi, and insist that proper retribution be administered to the transgressors, and that the girl be surrendered."

"It shall be done; it shall be so," said the Quatuorvir. Then, raising his hand to his mouth, and speaking behind it—not that in the roar of the wind such a precaution was necessary—he said to the pontiff: "My dear man, a magistrate has other matters to consider than pleasing the clubs. There is the prince over all, and he is on the way to Narbonese Gaul. It is whispered that he is favorably disposed towards this Nazarene sect."

"The Augustus would not desire to have the laws set at naught, and the sodalities are rich enough to pay to get access to him and make their complaint."

"Well, well, well! I cannot please all. I have to steer my course among shoals and rocks. Keep the question of Christianity in the background and charge on other grounds. That is my line. I will do my best to please all parties. We must have sport for the games. The rabble desire to have some one punished for spoiling their pet image. But, by the Twins, could not the poor god hold his own head on his shoulders? If he had been worth an *as*, he would have done so. But there, I nettle you. You shall be satisfied along with the rest. Bring up the prisoners: Quincta, widow of Aulus Harpinius Læto, first of all."

The mother of Perpetua was led forward in a condition of terror that rendered her almost unconscious, and unable to sustain herself.

"Quincta," said the magistrate, "have no fear for yourself. I have no desire to deal sharply with you; if you will inform us where is your daughter, you shall be dismissed forthwith."

"I do not know———" The poor woman could say no more.

"Give her a seat," ordered Petronius. Then to the prisoner: "Compose yourself. No doubt that, as a mother, you desire to screen your daughter, supposing that her life is menaced. No such thing, madame. I have spoken with the priestess, and with my good friend here, Lucius Smerius, chief pontiff, Augustal *flamen*, and public haruspex." He bowed to the priest at his side. "I am assured that the god, when he spoke, made no demand for a sacrifice. That is commuted. All he desires is that the young virgin should pass into his service, and be numbered among his priestesses."

"She will not consent," gasped Quincta.

"I hardly need to point out the honor and advantage offered her. The priestesses enjoy great favor with the people, have seats of honor at the theater, take a high position in all public ceremonies, and are maintained by rich endowments."

"She will never consent," repeated the mother.

"Of that we shall judge for ourselves. Where is the girl?"

"I do not know."

"How so?"

"She has been carried away from me; I know not whither."

"When the old ewe baas the lamb will bleat," said the Quatuorvir. "We shall find the means to make you produce her. Lady Quincta, my duty compels me to send you back to prison. You shall be allowed two days' respite. Unless, by the end of that time, you are able and willing to give us the requisite information, you will be put to the question, and I doubt not that a turn of the rack will refresh your memory and relax your tongue."

"I cannot tell what I do not know."

"Remove the woman."

The magistrate leaned back, and turning his head to the pontiff, said: "Did not your worthy father, Spurius, die of a surfeit of octopus? I had a supper off the legs last night, and they made me sleep badly; they are no better than marine leather." Then to the *vigiles*: "Bring forward Falerius Marcianus."

The deacon was conducted before the magistrate. He was pale, and his lips ashen and compressed. His dark eyes turned in every direction. He was looking for kinsmen and patron.

"You are charged, Falerius, with having broken the image of the god whom Nemausus delights to honor, and who is the reputed founder of the city. You conveyed his head to the house of Baudillas, and several witnesses have deposed that you made boast that you had committed the sacrilegious act of defacing the statue. What answer make you to this?"

Marcianus replied in a low voice.

"Speak up," said the magistrate; "I cannot hear thee, the wind blusters and bellows so loud." Aside to the pontiff Smerius he added: "And ever since that evil blast you wot of, I have suffered from a singing in my ears."

"I did it," said the deacon. Again he looked about him, but saw none to support him.

"Then," said the magistrate, "we shall at once conclude this matter. The outrage is too gross to be condoned or lightly punished. Even thy friends and kinsfolk have not appeared to speak for thee. Thy family has been one of dignity and authority in Nemausus. There have been members who have been clothed with the Quatuorvirate *de aerario* and have been accorded the use of a horse at public charge. Several have been decurions wearing the white toga and the purple stripe. This aggravates the impiety of your act. I sentence Cneius Falerius Marcianus, son of Marius Audolatius, of the Voltinian tribe, to be thrown to the beasts in the approaching show, and that his goods be confiscated, and that out of his property restitution be made, by which a new statue to the god Nemausus be provided, to be set up in the place of that injured by the same Cneius Falerius Marcianus."

The deacon made an attempt to speak. He seemed overwhelmed with astonishment and dismay at the sentence, so utterly unexpected in its severity. He gesticulated and cried out, but the Quatuorvir was cold and weary. He had pronounced a sentence that would startle all the town, and he thought he had done enough.

"Remove him at once," said he.

Then Petronius turned to the pontiff and said: "Now, my Smerius, what say you to this? Will not this content you and all the noisy rag-tag at your back?"

Next he commanded the rest of the prisoners to be brought forward together. This was a mixed number of poor persons, some women, some old men, boys, slaves and freedmen; none belonged to the upper class or even to that of the manufacturers and tradesmen.

"You are all dismissed," said the magistrate. "The imprisonment you have undergone will serve as a warning to you not to associate with image-breakers, not to enter into sodalities which have not received the sanction of Cæsar, and which are not compatible with the well-being and quiet of the city and are an element of disturbance in the empire. Let us hear no more of this pestilent nonsense. Go—worship what god ye will—only not Christos."

Then the lictors gathered around the Quatuorvir and the pontiff, who also rose, and extended his hand to assist the magistrate, who made wry faces as rheumatic twinges nipped his back.

"Come with me, Smerius," said the Quatuorvir, "I have done the best for you that lay in my power. I hate unnecessary harshness. But this fellow, Falerius Marcianus, has deserved the worst. If the old woman be put on the rack and squeak out, and Marcianus be devoured by beasts, the people will have their amusement, and none can say that I have acted with excessive rigor—and, my dear man—not a word has been said about Christianity. The cases have been tried on other counts, do you see?" he winked. "Will you breakfast with me? There are mullets from the Satera, stewed in white wine—confound those octopi!—I feel them still."

CHAPTER XXI

A MANUMISSION

"Blanda, what shall I do?"

Æmilius had withdrawn immediately after the interview in the citron-house, and Perpetua was left a prey to even greater distress of mind than before.

Accustomed to lean on her mother, she was now without support. She drew towards the female slave, who had a patient, gentle face, marked with suffering.

"Blanda, what shall I do?"

"Mistress, how can I advise? If you had been graciously pleased to take counsel of my master, he would have instructed you."

"Alack! what I desire is to find my mother. If, as I suppose, she is in concealment in Nemausus, he will be unable to discover her. No clue will be put into his hand. He will be regarded with suspicion. He will search; I do not doubt his good will, but he will not find. Those who know where my mother is will look on him with suspicion. O

Blanda, is there none in this house who believes, whom I could send to some of the Church?"

"Lady," answered the slave, "there be no Christians here. There is a Jew, but he entertains a deadly hate of such as profess to belong to this sect. To the rest one religion is as indifferent as another. Some swear by the White Ladies, some by Serapis, and there is one who talks much of Mithras, but who this god is I know not."

"If I am to obtain information it must be through some one who is to be trusted."

"Lady," said the woman-slave, "the master has given strict orders that none shall speak of you as having found a shelter here. Yet when slaves get together, by the Juno of the oaks, I believe men chatter and are greater magpies than we women; their tongues run away with them, especially when they taste wine. If one of the family were sent on this commission into the town, ten *sesterces* to an *as*, he would tell that you are here, and would return as owlish and ignorant as when he went forth. Men's minds are cudgels, not awls. If thou desirest to find out a thing, trust a woman, not a man."

"I cannot rest till I have news."

"There has been a great search made after

Christians, and doubtless she is, as thou sayest, in concealment, surely among friends. Have patience."

"But, Blanda, she is in an agony of mind as to what has become of me."

The slave-woman considered for awhile, and then said:

"There is a man who might help; he certainly can be relied on. He is of the strange sect I know, and he would do anything for me, and would betray no secrets."

"Who is that?"

"His name is Pedo, and he is the slave to Baudillas Macer, son of Carisius Adgonna, who has a house in the lower town."

"O Blanda!" exclaimed Perpetua, "it was from the house of Baudillas that I was enticed away." Then, after some hesitation, she added: "That house, I believe, was invaded by the mob; but I think my mother had first escaped."

"Lady, I have heard that Baudillas has been taken before the magistrate, and has been cast into the *robur*, because that in his house was found the head of the god; and it was supposed that he was guilty of the sacrilege, either directly or indirectly.

He that harbors a thief is guilty as the thief. I heard that yesterday. No news has since been received. I mistrust my power of reaching the town, of standing against the gale. Moreover, as the master has been imprisoned, it is not likely that the slave will be in the empty house. Yet, if thou wilt tarry till the gale be somewhat abated and the rain cease to fall in such a rush, I will do my utmost to assist thee. I will go to the town myself, and communicate with Pedo, if I can find him. He will trust me, poor fellow!"

"I cannot require thee to go forth in this furious wind," said Perpetua.

"And, lady, thou must answer to my master for me. Say that I went at thine express commands; otherwise I shall be badly beaten."

"Is thy master so harsh?"

"Oh, I am a slave. Who thinks of a slave any more than of an ass or a lapdog? It was through a severe scourging with the cat that I was brought to know Pedo."

"Tell me, how was that?"

"Does my lady care for matters that affect her slave?"

"Nay, good Blanda, we Christians know no difference between bond and free. All are the children of one God, who made man. Our master, though Lord of all, made Himself of no reputation, but took on Him the form of a servant; and was made subject for us."

"That is just how Pedo talks. We slaves have our notions of freedom and equality, and there is much tall talk in the servants' hall on the rights of man. But I never heard of a master or mistress holding such opinions."

"Nevertheless this doctrine is a principle of our religion. Listen to this; the words are those of one of our great teachers: 'There is neither Jew nor Greek, there is neither bond nor free, there is neither male nor female: for ye are all one in Christ Jesus.'"

"Was he a slave who said that?"

"No; he was a Roman citizen."

"That I cannot understand. Yet perhaps he spoke it at an election time, or when he was an advocate in the forum. It was a sentiment; very fine, smartly put, but not to be practiced."

"There, Blanda, you are wrong. We Christians do act upon this principle, and it forms a bond of union between us."

"Well, I understand it not. I have heard the slaves declaim among themselves, saying that they were as good as, nay, better than, their masters; but they never whispered such a thought where were their masters' ears, or they would have been soundly whipped. In the forum, when lawyers harangue, they say fine things of this sort; and when candidates are standing for election, either as a sevir or as a quatuorvir, all sorts of fine words fly about, and magnificent promises are made, but they are intended only to tickle ears and secure votes. None believe in them save the vastly ignorant and the very fools."

"Come, tell me about thyself and Pedo."

"Ah, lady, that was many years ago. I was then in the household of Helvia Secundilla, wife of Calvius Naso. On one occasion, because I had not brought her May-dew wherewith to bathe her face to remove sun-spots, she had me cruelly beaten. There were knucklebones knotted in the cat wherewith I was beaten. Thirty-nine lashes I received. I could not collect May-dew, for the sky was overcast and the herb was dry. But she regarded not my excuse. Tullia, my fellow-slave, was more sly. She filled a flask at a spring and pretended that she had gathered it off the grass, and that her fraud might not be detected, she egged her mistress on against me. I was chastised till my back was raw."

" Poor Blanda!"

" Aye, my back was one bleeding wound, and yet I was compelled to put on my garment and go forth again after May-dew. It was then that I encountered Pedo. I was in such pain that I walked sobbing, and my tears fell on the arid grass. He came to me, moved by compassion, and spoke kindly, and my heart opened, and I told him all. Then he gave me a flask filled with a water in which elder flowers had been steeped, and bade me wash my back therewith."

" And it healed thee?"

" It soothed the fever of my blood and the anguish of my wounds. They closed, and in a few days were cicatriced. But Pedo had been fellow-slave with a Jewish physician, and from him had learned the use of simples. My mistress found no advantage from the spring-water brought her as May-dew. Then I offered her some of the decoction given me by Pedo, and that had a marvelous effect on her freckles. Afterwards her treatment of me was kinder, and it was Tullia who received the whippings."

"And did you see more of Pedo?"

Blanda colored.

"Mistress, that was the beginning of our acquaintance. He was with a good master, Baudillas Macer, who, he said, would manumit him at any time. But, alas! what would that avail me? I remained in bondage. Ah, lady, Pedo regarded me with tenderness, and, indeed, I could have been happy with none other but him."

"He is old and lame."

"Ah, lady, I think the way he moves on his lame hip quite beautiful. I do not admire legs when one is of the same length as another—it gives a stiff uniformity not to my taste."

"And he is old?"

"Ripe, lady—full ripe as a fig in August. Sour fruit are unpleasant to eat. Young men are prigs and think too much of themselves."

"How long ago was it that this acquaintance began?"

"Five and twenty years. I trusted, when my master, Calvius Naso—he was so called because he really had a long nose, and my mistress was wont to tweak it—but there! I wander. I did think that he would have given me my freedom. In his illness I attended to him daily, nightly. I did not sleep, I was ever on the watch for him. As to my mistress, she was at her looking-glass, and using depilatory fluid on some hairs upon her chin, expecting shortly to be a widow. She did not concern herself about the master. He died, but left money only for the erection of a statue in the forum. Me he utterly forgot. Then my mistress sold me to the father of my present master. When he died also he manumitted eight slaves, but they were all men. His monument stands beside the road to Tolosa, with eight Phrygian caps sculptured on it, to represent the manumissions; but me—he forgot."

"Then, for all these five and twenty years you have cared for Pedo and desired to be united to him!"

"Yes, I longed for it greatly for twenty years, and so did he, poor fellow; but, after that, hope died. I have now no hope, no joy in life, no expectation of aught. Presently will come death, and death ends all."

"No, Blanda; that is not what we hold. We look for eternal life."

"For masters, not for slaves."

"For slaves as well as masters, and then God will wipe away all tears from our eyes."

"Alack, mistress. The power to hope is gone from me. In a wet season, when there is little sun, then the fruit mildews on the tree and drops off. When we were young we put forth the young fruit of hopes; but there has been no sun. They fall off, and the tree can bear no more."

"Blanda, if ever I have the power———"

"Oh, mistress, with my master you can do anything."

"Blanda, I do not know that I can ask him for this—thy freedom. But, if the opportunity offers, I certainly will not forget thee."

A slave appeared at the door and signed to Blanda, who, with an obeisance, asked leave to depart. The leave was given, and she left the room.

Presently she returned in great excitement, followed by Baudillas and Pedo, both drenched with rain and battered by the gale.

Perpetua uttered an exclamation of delight, and rushed to the deacon with extended arms.

"I pray, I pray, give me some news of my mother."

But he drew back likewise surprised, and replied with another question:

"The Lady Perpetua! And how come you to be here?"

"That I will tell later," answered the girl. "Now inform me as to my mother."

"Alas!" replied Baudillas, wiping the rain from his face, "the news is sad. She has been taken before Petronius, and has been consigned to prison."

"My mother is in prison!"

The deacon desired to say no more, but he was awkward at disguising his unwillingness to speak the whole truth. The eager eyes of the girl read the hesitation in his face.

"I beseech you," she urged, "conceal nothing from me."

"I have told you, she is in jail."

"On what charge? Who has informed against her?"

"I was not in the court when she was tried. I know very little. I was near the town, waiting about, and I got scraps of information from some of our people, and from Pedo, who went into the city."

"Then you do know. Answer me truly. Tell me all."

"I—I was in prison myself, but escaped through the aid of Pedo. I tarried in an old kiln. He advised that I should come on here, where he had friends. Dost thou know that Marcianus has been sentenced? He will win that glorious crown which I have lost. I—I, unworthy, I fled, when it might have been mine. Yet, God forgive me! I am not ungrateful to Pedo. Marcianus said I was a coward, and unfit for the Kingdom of God; that I should be excluded because I had turned back. God forgive me!"

Suddenly Perpetua laid hold of Baudillas by both arms, and so gripped him that the water oozed between her fingers and dropped on the floor.

"I adjure thee, by Him in whom we both believe, answer me truly, speak fully. Is my mother retained in prison till I am found?"

The deacon looked down nervously, uncomfortably, and shuffled from foot to foot.

"Understand," said he, after a long silence, "all I learned is by hearsay. I really know nothing for certain."

"I suffer more by your silence than were I to be told the truth, be the truth never so painful."

"Have I not said it? The Lady Quincta is in prison."

"Is that all?"

Again he maintained an embarrassed silence.

"It matters not," said Perpetua firmly. "I will my own self find out what has taken place. I shall return to Nemausus on foot, and immediately. I will deliver myself up to the magistrate and demand my mother's release."

"You must not go—the weather is terrible."

"I shall—nothing can stay me. I shall go, and go alone, and go at once."

"There is no need for such haste. It is not till to-morrow that Quincta will be put on the rack."

"On the rack!"

"Fool that I am! I have uttered what I should have kept secret."

"It is said. My resolve is formed. I return to Nemausus."

"Then," said the deacon, "I will go with thee."

"There is no need. I will take Blanda."

"I will go. A girl, a young girl shames me. I run away from death, and she offers herself to the sword. Marcianus said I was a renegade. I will not be thought to have denied my Master—to have fled from martyrdom."

"Then," said Perpetua, "I pray thee this—first give freedom unto Pedo."

Baudillas administered a slight stroke on the cheek to his slave, and said:

"Go; thou art discharged from bondage."

CHAPTER XXII

THE ARENA

The games that were to be given in the amphitheater of Nemausus on the nones of March were due to a bequest of Domitius Afer, the celebrated, or rather infamous, informer and rhetorician, who had brought so many citizens of Rome to death during the principate of Tiberius. He had run great risk himself under Caligula, but had escaped by a piece of adroit flattery. In dying he bequeathed a large sum out of his ill-gotten gains—the plunder of those whom he had destroyed, and whose families he had ruined—to be expended in games in the amphitheater on the nones of March, for the delectation of the citizens, and to keep his memory green in his native city.

The games were to last two days. On the first there would be contests with beasts, and on the second a water combat, when the arena would be flooded and converted into a lake.

Great anxiety was entertained relative to the

weather. Unless the mistral ceased and the rain passed away, it would be impossible for the sports to be held. It was true that the entire oval could be covered in by curtains and mats, stretched between poles, but this contrivance was intended as shelter against sun and not rain. Moreover, the violence of the wind had rendered it quite impossible to extend the curtains.

The town was in the liveliest excitement. The man guilty of having mutilated the statue had been sentenced to be cast to the beasts, and this man was no vulgar criminal out of the slums, but belonged to one of the superior " orders."

That a great social change had taken place in the province, and that the freedmen had stepped into power and influence, to the displacement of their former masters, was felt by the descendants of the first Ægypto-Greek colonists, and by the relics of the Gaulish nobility, but they hardly endured to admit the fact in words. The exercise of the rights of citizenship, the election of the officials, the qualification for filling the superior secular and religious offices, belonged to the decurion or noble families. Almost the sole office open to those below was that of the seviri; and yet even in elections the freedmen were beginning to exhibit a power of control.

Now, one of the old municipal families was to be humbled by a member being subjected to the degradation of death in the arena, and none of the Falerii ventured to raise a voice in his defence, so critical did they perceive the situation to be. The sodality of the Augustals in conclave had determined that an example was to be made of Marcianus, and had made this plain to the magistrates. They had even insisted on the manner of his execution. His death would be a plain announcement to the decurion class that its domination was at an end. The ancient patrician and plebeian families of Rome had been extinguished in blood, and their places filled by a new nobility of army factors and money-lenders. A similar revolution had taken place in the provinces by less bloody means. There, the transfer of power was due largely to the favor of the prince accorded to the freedmen.

In the Augustal colleges everywhere, the Cæsar had a body of devoted adherents, men without nationality, with no historic position, no traditions of past independence; men, moreover, who were shrewd enough to see that by combination they would eventually be able to wrest the control of the municipal government from those who had hitherto exercised it.

The rumor spread rapidly that a fresh entertainment was to be provided. The damsel who had been rescued from the basin of Nemausus had surrendered herself in order to obtain the release of her mother; and the magistrate in office, Petronius Atacinus, out of consideration for the good people of the town, whom he loved, and out of reverence for the gods who had been slighted, had determined that she should be produced in the arena, and there obliged publicly to sacrifice, and then to be received into the priesthood. Should she, however, prove obdurate, then she would be tortured into compliance.

Nor was this all. Baudillas Macer, the last scion of a decayed Volcian family, who had been cast into the pit of the *robur*, but had escaped, was also to be brought out and executed, as having assisted in the rescue of Perpetua from the fountain, but chiefly for having connived at the crime of Falerius Marcianus.

To the general satisfaction, the wind fell as suddenly as it had risen, and that on the night preceding the sports. The weather remained bitterly cold, and the sky was dark with clouds that seemed ready to burst. Not a ray of sunlight traveled across the arena and climbed the stages of the amphitheater. The day might have been one in November, and the weather that encountered on the northern plains of Germania.

The townsfolk, and the spectators from the country, came provided against the intemperance of the weather, wrapped in their warmest mantles, which they drew as hoods over their heads. Slaves arrived, carrying boxes with perforated tops, that contained glowing charcoal, so that their masters and mistresses might keep their feet warm whilst attending the games. Some carried cushions for the seats, others wolf-skin rugs to throw over the knees of the well-to-do spectators.

The ranges of the great oval were for the most part packed with spectators. The topmost seats were full long before the rest. The stone benches were divided into tiers. At the bottom, near the *podium* or breastwork confining the arena, were those for the municipal dignitaries, for the priests, and for certain strangers to whom seats had been granted by decree of the town council. Here might be read,

"Forty seats decreed to the navigators of the Rhône and Saone;" at another part of the circumference, "Twenty-five places appointed to the navigators of the Ardèche and the Ouvèze."

Above the ranges of seats set apart for the officials and guests were those belonging to the decurions and knights, the nobility and gentry of the town and little republic. The third range was that allotted to the freedmen and common townsfolk and peasants from the country, and the topmost stage was abandoned to be occupied by slaves alone. At one end of the ellipse sat the principal magistrates close to the *podium* at one end, and at the other the master of the games and his attendants, the prefect of the watch and of the firemen.

Two doors, one at each end, gave access to the arena, or means of exit. One was that of the *vivarium*, whence the gladiators and prisoners issued from a large chamber under the seats and feet of the spectators. The other door was that which conducted to the *libitinum*, into which were cast the corpses of men and the carcasses of beasts that had perished in the games.

Immediately below the seat of the principal magistrates and of the pontiffs was a little altar, on the breastwork about the arena, with a statue of Nemausus above it; and a priest stood at the side to keep the charcoal alight, and to serve the incense to such as desired to do homage to the god.

It was remarked that the attendance in the reserved seats of the decurions was meager. Such as were connected with the Falerian family by blood or marriage made it a point to absent themselves; others stayed away because huffed at the insolence of the freedmen, and considering that the sentence passed on Marcianus was a slight cast on their order.

On the other hand, the freedmen crowded to the show in full force, and not having room to accommodate themselves and their families in the zone allotted to them, some audaciously threw themselves over the barriers of demarcation and were followed by others, and speedily flooded the benches of the decurions.

When the magistrates arrived, preceded by their lictors, all in the amphitheater rose, and the Quatuor-viri bowed to the public. Each took a pinch from the priest, who extended a silver shell containing aromatic gums, and cast it on the fire, some gravely, Petronius with a flippant gesture. Then the latter turned to the Augustal *flamen*, saying: "To the god Augustus and the divine Julia (Livia)," and he threw some more grains on the charcoal.

"Body of Bacchus!" said he, as he took his seat, "a little fizzling spark such as that may please the gods, but does not content me. I wish I had a roaring fire at which, like a babe out of its bath, I could spread my ten toes and as many fingers. Such a day as this is! With cold weather I cannot digest my food properly. I feel a lump in me as did Saturn when his good Rhea gave him a meal of stones. I am full of twinges. By Vulcan and his bellows! if it had not been for duty I would have been at home adoring the Lares and Penates. These shows are for the young and warm-blooded. The arms of my chair send a chill into my marrow-bones. What comes first? Oh! a contest with a bull. Well, I shall curl up and doze like a marmot. Wake me, good Smerius, when the next portion of the entertainment begins."

A bull was introduced, and a gladiator was employed to exasperate and play with the beast. He waved a garment before its eyes, then drove a sharp instrument into its flank, and when the beast turned, he nimbly leaped out of the way. When pursued he ran, then turned sharply, put his hands on the back of the bull, and leaped over it.

The people cheered, but they had seen the performance so often repeated that they speedily tired of such poor sport. The bull was accordingly dispatched. Horses were introduced and hooked to the carcass, which was rapidly drawn out. Then entered attendants of the amphitheater, who strewed sand where the blood had been spilt, bowed and retired.

Thereupon the jailer threw open the gates of the *vivarium* and brought forth the prisoners. These consisted of the taverner who had murdered his guests, the manumitted slave who had robbed his master, Baudillas, Marcianus and Perpetua.

A thrill of cruel delight ran through the concourse of spectators. Now something was about to be shown them, harrowing to the feelings, gratifying to the ferocity that is natural to all men, and is expelled, not at all by civilization, but by divine grace only.

It enhanced the pleasure of the spectators that criminals should witness the death of their fellows. Eyes scanned their features, observed whether they turned sick and faint, whether they winced, or whether they remained cool and callous. This gave a cruel zest to their enjoyment.

A bear was produced. Dogs were set on him, and he was worried till he shook off his torpor and was worked into fury. Then, at a sign from the manager of the games, the dogs were called off, and the man who had murdered his guests was driven forward towards the incensed beast.

The fellow was sullen, and gave no token of fear. He folded his arms, leaned against the marble *podium*, and looked contemptuously around him at the occupants of the tiers of seats.

The bear, relieved from his aggressors, seemed indisposed to notice the man.

Then the spectators roared to the criminal, bidding him invite the brute against himself. It was a strange fact that often in these horrible exhibitions a man condemned to fight with the beasts allowed himself a brief display of vanity, and sought to elicit the applause of the spectators by his daring conduct to the animal that was to mangle and kill him.

But the ill-humored fellow would not give this pleasure to the onlookers.

Then the master of the sports signed to the attendants to goad the bear. They obeyed, and he turned and growled and struck at them, but would not touch the man designed to be hugged by him.

After many vain attempts, amidst the hooting and roar of the people, a sign was made. Some gladiators leaped in, and with their swords dispatched the taverner.

The spectators were indignant. They had been shown no sport, only a common execution. They were shivering with cold; some grumbled, and said that this was childish stuff to witness which was not worth the discomfort of the exposure. Then, as with one voice, rose the yell: "The wolves! send in the wolves! Marcianus to the wolves!"

The master of the games dispatched a messenger to the Quatuorvir who was then the acting magistrate. He nodded to what was said, waved his hand in the direction of the master's box, and the latter sent an attendant to the keeper of the beasts.

The jailer-executioner at once grasped the deacon Falerius Marcianus by the shoulders, bade him descend some steps and enter the arena.

Marcianus was deadly white. He shrank with disgust from the spot where the soil was drenched with the blood of the taverner, and which was not as yet strewn over with fresh sand. He cast a furtive look at the altar, then made an appealing gesture to the magistrate.

"Come here, Cneius Marcianus," said Petronius. "You belong to a respectable and ancient family. You have been guilty of an infamous deed that has brought disgrace on your entire order. See how many absent themselves this day on that account! Your property is confiscated, you are sentenced to death. Yet I give you one chance. Sacrifice to the gods and blaspheme Christ. I do not promise you life if you do this. You must appeal to the people. If they see you offer incense, they will know that you have renounced the Crucified. Then I will put the question to their decision. If they hold up their thumbs you will live. Consider, it is a chance; it depends, not on me, but on their humor. Will you sacrifice?"

Marcianus looked at the mighty hoop of faces. He saw that the vast concourse was thrilled with expectation; a notion crossed the mind of one of the freedmen that Marcianus was being given a means of escape, and he shouted words that, though audible and intelligible to those near, were not to be caught by such as were distant. But the purport of his address was understood, and produced a deafening, a furious roar of remonstrance.

"I will not sacrifice," said the deacon; "I am a Christian."

Then Petronius Atacinus raised his hand, partly to assure the spectators that he was not opposing their wishes, partly as a signal to the master of the games.

Instantly a low door in the barrier was opened, and forth rushed a howling pack of wolves. When they had reached the center of the arena, they stood for a moment snuffing, and looked about them in questioning attitudes. Some, separating from the rest, ran with their snouts against the ground to where the recent blood had been spilt. But, all at once, a huge gray wolf, that led the pack, uttered a howl, and made a rush and a leap towards Marcianus; and the rest followed.

The sight was too terrible for the deacon to contemplate it unmoved. He remained but for an instant as one frozen, and then with a cry he started and ran round the ellipse, and the whole gray pack tore after him. Now and then, finding that they gained on him, he turned with threatening gestures that cowed the brutes; but this was for a moment only. Their red eyes, their gleaming teeth filled the wretched man with fresh terror, and again he ran.

The spectators clapped their hands—some stood up on their seats and laughed in ecstasy of enjoyment. Once, twice he made the circuit of the arena; and his pace, if possible, became quicker. The delight of the spectators became an intoxication. It was exquisite. Fear in the flying man became frantic. His breath, his strength were failing. Then suddenly he halted, half turned, and ran to the foot of the barrier before the seat of the Quatuor-viri, and extended his hand: "Give me the incense! I worship Nemausus! I adore Augustus! I renounce Christ!"

At the same moment the old monster wolf had seized him from behind. The arms of the deacon were seen for an instant in the air. The spectators stamped and danced and cheered—the dense gray mass of writhing, snarling beasts closed over the spot where Marcianus had fallen!

CHAPTER XXIII

THE CLOUD-BREAK

The acting magistrate turned to his fellow-quatuorvir, charged with co-ordinate judicial authority, on the left, and said: "Your nose is leaden-purple in hue."

"No marvel, in this cold. I ever suffer there with the least frost. My ear lobes likewise are seats of chilblain."

"In this climate! Astonishing! If it had been in Britain, or in Germany, it might have been expected."

"My brother-magistrate," said Vibius Fuscianus, "I believe that here in the south we are more sensible to frost than are those who live under hyperborean skies. There they expect cold, and take precautions accordingly. Here the blasts fall on us unawares. We groan and sigh till the sun shines out, and then forget our sufferings. Who but fools would be here to-day? Look above. The clouds hang low, and are so dark that we may expect to be pelted with hail."

"Aye," laughed Petronius, "as big as the pebbles that strew the Crau wherewith Hercules routed the Ligurians. Well; it is black as an eclipse. I will give thee a hint, Vibius mine! I have made my slave line this marble seat with hot bricks. They are comforting to the spine, the very column of life. Presently he will be here with another supply. You see we are not all fools. Some do make provision against the cold."

"I wish I had thought of this before."

"That is precisely the wish that crossed the mind of the poor wretch whom the wolves have finished. He postponed his renunciation of Christ till just too late."

Then Lucius Petronius yawned, stretched himself, and signed that the freedman who had robbed the master who had manumitted him, should be delivered to a panther.

The wolves were with difficulty chased out of the arena, and then all was prepared for this next exhibition. It was brief. The beast was hungry, and the criminal exposed made little effort to resist. Next came the turn of Baudillas.

Without raising himself in his seat, the Quatuorvir said languidly: "You broke out of prison, you were charged with aiding and abetting sacrilege. You refused to sacrifice to the genius of the Emperor. Well, if you will cast a few grains of incense in the fire, I will let you depart."

"I cannot forswear Christ," said Baudillas with a firmness that surprised none so much as himself. But, indeed, the fall of Marcianus, so far from drawing him along into the same apostasy, had caused a recoil in his soul. To hear his fellow-ministrant deny Christ, to see him extend his hands for the incense—that inspired him with an indignation which gave immense force to his resolution. The Church had been dishonored, the ministry disgraced in Marcianus. Oh, that they might not be thus humbled in himself!

"Baudillas Macer," said the magistrate, "take advice, and be speedy in making your election; your fellow, who has just furnished a breakfast to the wolves, hesitated a moment too long, and so lost his life. By the time he had resolved to act as a wise man and a good citizen, not the gods themselves could deliver him. *Flamen,* hand the shell with the grains to this sensible fellow."

"I cannot offer sacrifice."

"You are guilty of treason against Cæsar if you

refuse to sacrifice to his genius. Never mind about Nemausus, whose image is there. Say—the genius of Cæsar, and you are quit."

"I am his most obedient subject."

"Then offer a libation or some frankincense."

"I cannot. I pray daily to God for him."

"A wilful man is like a stubborn ass. There is naught for him but the stick. I can do no more. I shall sentence you."

"I am ready to die for Christ."

"Then lead him away. The sword!"

The deacon bowed. "I am unworthy of shedding my blood for Christ," he said, and his voice, though low, was firm.

Then he looked around and saw the Bishop Castor in the zone allotted to the citizens and knights. Baudillas crossed his arms on his breast and knelt on the sand, and the bishop, rising from his seat, extended his hand in benediction.

He, Castor, had not been called to sacrifice. He had not courted death, but he had not shrunk from it. He had not concealed himself, nevertheless he had been passed over.

Then the deacon, with firm step, walked into the center of the arena and knelt down.

In another moment his head was severed from the body.

The attendants immediately removed every trace of the execution, and now arrived the moment for which all had looked with impatience.

The magistrate said: "Bring forward Perpetua, daughter of Aulus Harpinius Læto, that has lived."

At once Æmilius sprang into the arena and advanced before Petronius.

"Suffer me to act as her advocate," said he in an agitated voice. "You know me, I am Lentulus Varo."

"I know you very well by repute, Æmilius," answered the Quatuorvir; "but I think there is no occasion now for your services. This is not a court of justice in which your forensic eloquence can be heard, neither is this a case to be adjudicated upon, and calling for defence. The virgin was chosen by lot to be given to the god Nemausus, and was again demanded by him speaking at midnight, after she had been rescued from his fountain, if I mistake not, by you. Your power of interference ceased there. Now, she is accused of nothing. She is reconsigned to the god, whose she is."

"I appeal to Cæsar."

"If I were to allow the appeal, would that avail thy client? But it is no case in which an appeal is justifiable. The god is merciful. He does not exact the life of the damsel, he asks only that she enter into his service and be a priestess at his shrine, that she pour libations before his altar, and strew rose leaves on his fountain. Think you that the Cæsar will interfere in such a matter? Think you that, were it to come before him, he would forbid this? But ask thy client if the appeal be according to her desire."

Perpetua shook her head.

"No, she is aware that it would be profitless. If thou desirest to serve her, then use thy persuasion and induce her to do sacrifice."

"Sir," said Æmilius in great agitation, "how can she become the votary of a god in whom she does not believe?"

"Oh, as to that," answered the Quatuorvir, "it is a formality, nothing more; a matter of incense and rose leaves. As to *belief*," he turned to his fellow-magistrate, and said, laughing, "listen to this man. He talks of belief, as though that were a necessary ingredient in worship! Thou, with thy plum-colored nose, hast thou full faith in Æsculapius to cure thee even of a chilblain?"

Fuscianus shrugged his shoulders. "I hate all meddlers with usages that are customary. I hate them as I do a bit of grit in my salad. I put them away."

The populace became impatient, shouted and stamped. Some, provided with empty gourds, in which were pebbles, rattled them, and made a strange sound as of a hailstorm. Others clacked together pieces of pottery. The magistrate turned to the pontiff on his right and said: "We believe with all our hearts in the gods when we do sacrifice! Oh, mightily, I trow." Then he laughed again. The priest looked grave for a moment, and then he laughed also.

"Come now," said Lucius Petronius to the young lawyer, "to this I limit thy interference. Stand by the girl and induce her to yield. By the Bowbearer! young men do not often fail in winning the consent of girls when they use their best blandishments. It will be a scene for the stage. You have plenty of spectators."

"Suffer me also to stand beside her," said the slave-woman Blanda, who had not left Perpetua.

"By all means. And if you two succeed, none will be better content than myself. I am not one who would wish a fair virgin a worse fate than to live and be merry and grow old. Ah me! old age!"

Again the multitude shouted and rattled pumpkins.

"We are detaining the people in the cold," said the presiding magistrate; "the sports move sluggishly as does our blood." Then, aside to Fuscianus, "My bricks are becoming sensibly chilled. I require a fresh supply." Then to the maiden: "Hear me, Perpetua, daughter of Harpinius Læto that was—we and the gods, or the gods and we, are indisposed to deal harshly. Throw a few crumbs of incense on the altar, and you shall pass at once up those steps to the row of seats where sit the white-robed priestesses with their crowns. I shall be well content."

"That is a thing I cannot do," said Perpetua firmly.

"Then we shall have to make you," said the magistrate in hard tones. He was angry, vexed. "You will prove more compliant when you have been extended on the rack. Let her be disrobed and tortured."

Then descended into the arena two young men, who bowed to the magistrate, solicited leave, and drew forth styles or iron pens and tablets covered with wax. These were the scribes of the Church employed everywhere to take down a record of the last interrogatory of a martyr. Such records were called the "Acts." Of them great numbers have been preserved, but unhappily rarely unfalsified. The simplicity of the acts, the stiffness of style, the adsence of all miraculous incident, did not suit the taste of mediæval compilers, and they systematically interpolated the earlier acts with harrowing details and records of marvels. Nevertheless, a certain number of these acts remain uncorrupted, and with regard to the rest it is not difficult to separate in them that which is fictitious from that which is genuine. Such notaries were admitted to the trials and executions with as much indifference as would be newspaper reporters nowadays.

Again, with the sweat of anguish breaking out on his brow, Æmilius interposed.

"I pray your mercy," he said; "let the sentence be still further modified. Suffer the damsel to be relieved of becoming a priestess. Let her become my wife, and I swear that I will make over my estate of Ad Fines to the temple of the god Nemausus, with the villa upon it, and statues and works of art."

"That is an offer to be entertained by the priesthood and not by me. Boy—hot bricks! and be quick about removing those which have become almost cold."

A pause ensued whilst the proposal of Æmilius was discussed between the chief priestess of the fountain and the Augustal *flamen* and the other pontiffs.

The populace became restless, impatient, noisy. They shouted, hooted; called out that they were tired of seeing nothing.

"Come," said Petronius, "I cannot further delay proceedings."

"We consent," said the chief pontiff.

"That is well."

Then Æmilius approached Perpetua, and entreated her to give way. To cast a few grains on the charcoal meant nothing; it was a mere movement of the hand, a hardly conscious muscular act, altogether out of comparison with the results. Such compliance would give her life, happiness, and would place her in a position to do vast good, and he assured her that his whole life would be devoted to her service.

"I cannot," she said, looking Æmilius full in the face. "Do not think me ungrateful; my heart overflows for what you have done for me, but I cannot deny my Christ."

Again he urged her. Let her consent and he— even he would become a Christian.

"No," said she, "not at that price. You would be in heart for ever estranged from the faith."

"To the rack! Lift her on to the little horse. Domitius Afer left his bequest to the city in order that we should be amused, not befooled," howled the spectators.

Executioners, do your duty," said the magistrate. "But if she cry out, let her off. She will sacrifice. Only to the first hole—mind you. If that does not succeed, well, then, we shall try sharper means."

And now the little horse was set up in the midst of the arena, and braziers of glowing charcoal were planted beside it; in the fire rested crooks and pincers to get red hot.

The "little horse" was a structure of timber. Two planks were set edgeways with a wheel between them at each end. The structure stood on four legs, two at each extremity, spreading at the base. Halfway down, between these legs, at the ends, was a roller, furnished with levers that passed through them. A rope was attached to the ankles, another to the wrists of the person extended on the back of the "horse," and this rope was strained over the pulleys by means of the windlasses. The levers could be turned to any extent, so as, if required, to wrench arms and legs from their sockets.

And now ensued a scene that refuses description. "We are made a spectacle unto men and angels," said the apostle, and none could realize how true were the words better than those who lived in times of persecution. Before that vast concourse the modest Christian maiden was despoiled of her raiment and was stretched upon the rack—swung between the planks.

Æmilius felt his head swim and his heart contract. What could he do? Again he entreated, but she shook her head, yet turned at his voice and smiled.

Then the executioners threw themselves on the levers, and a hush as of death fell on the multitude. Twenty thousand spectators looked on, twice that number of eyes were riveted on the frail girl undergoing this agony. Bets had been made on her constancy, bandied about, taken, and booked. Castor stood up, with face turned to heaven, and extended arms, praying.

The creaking of the windlass was audible; then rang out a sharp cry of pain.

Immediately the cords were relaxed and the victim lowered to the ground. Blanda threw a mantle over her.

"She will sacrifice," said Æmilius; "take off the cords."

The executioners looked to the magistrate. He nodded, and they obeyed. The bonds were rapidly removed from her hands and feet.

"Blanda, sustain her!" commanded Æmilius, and he on one side, with his arm round the sinking, quivering form, and the slave-woman on the other, supported Perpetua. Her feet dragged and traced a furrow in the sand; they were numbed and powerless through the tension of the cords that had been knotted about the ankles. Æmilius and Blanda drew her towards the altar.

"I cannot! I will not sacrifice! I am a Christian. I believe in Christ! I love Christ!"

"Perpetua," said Æmilius in agitated tones,

"your happiness and mine depend on compliance. For all I have done for you, if you will not for your own sake—consent to this. Here! I will hold your hand. Nay, it is I who will strew the incense, and make it appear as though it were done by you. Priest! The shell with the grains."

"Spare me! I cannot!" gasped the girl, struggling in his arms. "I cannot be false to my Christ —for all that He has done for me."

"You shall. I must constrain you." He set his teeth, knitted his brow. All his muscles were set in desperation. He strove to force her hand to the altar.

"Shame on thee!" sobbed she. "Thou art more cruel than the torturer, more unjust than the judge."

It was so. Æmilius felt that she was right. They did but insult and rack a frail body, and he did violence to the soul within.

The people hooted and roared, and brandished their arms threateningly. "We will not be balked! We are being treated to child's play."

"Take her back to the rack. Apply the fire," ordered the Quatuorvir.

The executioners reclaimed her. She offered no resistance. Æmilius staggered to the *podium* and grasped the marble top with one hand.

She was again suspended on the little horse. Again the windlass creaked. The crowd listened, held its breath, men looked in each other's eyes, then back to the scene of suffering. Not a sound; not a cry; no, not even a sigh. She bore all.

"Try fire!" ordered the magistrate.

Æmilius had covered his face. He trembled. He would have shut his ears as he did his eyes, could he have done so. Verily, the agony of his soul was as great as the torture of her body. But there was naught to be heard—an ominous stillness, only the groaning of the windlass, and now and then a word from one executioner to his fellow.

At every creak of the wheel a quiver went through the frame of Æmilius. He listened with anguish of mind for a cry. The populace held its breath; it waited. There was none. Into her face he dared not look. But the twenty thousand spectators stared—and saw naught save lips moving in prayer.

And now a mighty wonder occurred.

The dense cloud that filled the heavens began softly, soundlessly, to discharge its burden. First came, scarce noticed, sailing down, a few large white flakes like fleeces of wool. Then they came fast, faster, ever faster. And now it was as though a white bridal veil had been let down out of heaven to hide from the eyes of the ravening multitude the spectacle of the agony of Christ's martyr. None could see across the arena; soon none could see obscurely into it. The snowflakes fell thick and dense, they massed as a white cornice on the parapet, they dropped on every head, they whitened the bloodstained, trampled sand. And all fled before the snow. First went a few in twos or threes; then whole rows stood up, and through the vomitories the multitude poured—freedmen, slaves, knights, ladies, *flamines*, magistrates; none could stand against the descending snow.

"Cast her down!" This was the last command issued by Petronius as he rose from his seat. The executioners were glad to escape. They relaxed the ropes, and threw their victim on the already white ground.

Still thick and fast fell the fleeces. Blanda had cast a mantle of wool over the prostrate girl, but out of heaven descended a pall, whiter than fuller on earth can bleach, and buried the woolen cloak and the extended quivering limbs. Beside her, in the snow, knelt Æmilius. He held her hand in one of his. She looked him in the face and smiled. Then she said: "Give to Blanda her liberty."

He could not speak. He signed that it should be so.

Then she said: "I have prayed for thee—on the rack, in the fire—that the light may shine into thy heart."

She closed her eyes.

Still he held her hand, and with the other gently brushed away the snowflakes as they fell on her pure face. Oh wondrous face! Face above the dream of the highest Greek artist!

Thus passed an hour—thus a second.

Then suddenly the clouds parted, and the sun poured down a flood of glory over the dazzling white oval field, in the midst of which lay a heap of whiteness, and on a face as of alabaster, inanimate, and on a kneeling, weeping man, still with reverent finger sweeping away the last snowflakes from eyelash, cheek and hair, and who felt as if he could thus look, and kneel, and weep for ever.*

---

* The incident of the fall of snow occurring at the martyrdom of a virgin saint is no picture of the author's imagination. It occurred at the passion of S. Eulalia of Merida, in A.D. 303, and is commemorated in the hymn on her by Prudentius.

CHAPTER XXIV

CREDO

Many days had passed. All was calm in Nemausus. The games were over.

The day succeeding that we have described was warm and spring-like. The sun shone brilliantly. Every trace of the snow had disappeared, and the water-fight in the amphitheater had surpassed the expectations of the people. They had enjoyed themselves heartily.

All had returned to its old order. The wool merchant took fresh commands, and sent his travelers into the Cebennæ to secure the winter fleeces. The woman who had the flower-shop sold garlands as fast as she could weave them. The potter spread out a fresh collection of his wares and did a good business with them.

The disturbances that had taken place were no more spoken about. The deaths of Marcianus, Baudillas and Perpetua hardly occupied any thoughts, save only those of their relatives and the Christians.

The general public had seen a show, and the show over, they had other concerns to occupy them.

Now both Pedo and Blanda were free, and the long tarrying was over. They had loved when young, they came together in the autumn of their lives.

In the heart of the Church of Nemausus there was not forgetfulness of its heroes.

If the visitor at the present day to Nîmes will look about him, he will find two churches, both recently rebuilt, in place of, and on the site of, very ancient places of worship, and the one bears the name of St. Baudille. If he inquire of the sacristan, "Mais qui, donc, était-il, ce saint?" then the answer given him will be: "Baudillas was a native of Nîmes, a deacon, and a martyr."

If he ask further, "But when?" Then the sacristan will probably reply with a shrug: "Mais, monsieur; qui sait?"

In another part of the town is a second church, glowing internally with color from its richly painted windows, and this bears the name of Ste. Perpetue.

Does the visitor desire to be told whether it has been erected in honor and in commemoration of the celebrated African martyrs Felicitas and Perpetua, or of some local virgin saint who shed her blood for Christ, then let him again inquire of the sacristan.

What his answer will be I cannot say.

The Bishop Castor remained much in his house. He grieved that he had not been called to witness to the faith that was in him. But he was a humble man, and he said to himself: "Such was the will of God, and that sufficeth me."

One evening he was informed that a man, who would not give his name, desired to speak with him.

He ordered that he should be introduced.

When the visitor entered, Castor recognized Æmilius, but the man was changed. Lines of thought and of sorrow marked his face, that bore other impress as well of the travail of his soul within him. He seemed older, his face more refined than before, there was less of carnal beauty, and something spiritual that shone out of his eyes.

The bishop warmly welcomed him.

Then said Æmilius in a low tone, "I am come to thee for instruction. I know but little, yet what I know of Christ I believe. He is not dead, He liveth; He is a power; mighty is faith, and mighty is the love that He inspires. *Credo.*"

Trieste

Trieste Publishing has a massive catalogue of classic book titles. Our aim is to provide readers with the highest quality reproductions of fiction and non-fiction literature that has stood the test of time. The many thousands of books in our collection have been sourced from libraries and private collections around the world.

The titles that Trieste Publishing has chosen to be part of the collection have been scanned to simulate the original. Our readers see the books the same way that their first readers did decades or a hundred or more years ago. Books from that period are often spoiled by imperfections that did not exist in the original. Imperfections could be in the form of blurred text, photographs, or missing pages. It is highly unlikely that this would occur with one of our books. Our extensive quality control ensures that the readers of Trieste Publishing's books will be delighted with their purchase. Our staff has thoroughly reviewed every page of all the books in the collection, repairing, or if necessary, rejecting titles that are not of the highest quality. This process ensures that the reader of one of Trieste Publishing's titles receives a volume that faithfully reproduces the original, and to the maximum degree possible, gives them the experience of owning the original work.

We pride ourselves on not only creating a pathway to an extensive reservoir of books of the finest quality, but also providing value to every one of our readers. Generally, Trieste books are purchased singly - on demand, however they may also be purchased in bulk. Readers interested in bulk purchases are invited to contact us directly to enquire about our tailored bulk rates. Email: customerservice@triestepublishing.com

You May Also Like

Some Modern Difficulties: Nine Lectures

S. Baring-Gould

ISBN: 9780649707751
Paperback: 204 pages
Dimensions: 6.14 x 0.43 x 9.21 inches
Language: eng

The Silver Store, Collected from Mediaeval Christian and Jewish Mines

S. Baring-Gould

ISBN: 9780649704996
Paperback: 224 pages
Dimensions: 6.14 x 0.47 x 9.21 inches
Language: eng

www.triestepublishing.com

You May Also Like

The Preacher's Pocket: A Pocket of Sermons

S. Baring-Gould

ISBN: 9780649678594
Paperback: 270 pages
Dimensions: 6.14 x 0.57 x 9.21 inches
Language: eng

One Hundred Sermon Sketches for Extempore Preachers

S. Baring-Gould

ISBN: 9780649661985
Paperback: 240 pages
Dimensions: 6.14 x 0.50 x 9.21 inches
Language: eng

www.triestepublishing.com

You May Also Like

Abraham Lincoln: The Practical Mystic

Francis Grierson

ISBN: 9780649438075
Paperback: 116 pages
Dimensions: 5.5 x 0.24 x 8.25 inches
Language: eng

A brief history of political parties in the United States

J. L. Pickard

ISBN: 9780649314775
Paperback: 70 pages
Dimensions: 6.14 x 0.14 x 9.21 inches
Language: eng

www.triestepublishing.com

You May Also Like

A Calendar of Sonnets

Helen Jackson

ISBN: 9780649265701
Paperback: 60 pages
Dimensions: 6.14 x 0.12 x 9.21 inches
Language: eng

A Calendar of Sonnets

Helen Jackson

ISBN: 9780649323432
Paperback: 64 pages
Dimensions: 6.14 x 0.13 x 9.21 inches
Language: eng

Find more of our titles on our website. We have a selection of thousands of titles that will interest you. Please visit

www.triestepublishing.com

Lightning Source UK Ltd.
Milton Keynes UK
UKOW06f0933231017

311488UK00005B/717/P